FICTION
GREGORY, JACK.
BLACK OUT

Taking his clipboard with him, Jim began picking his way carefully through the rubble of the old building. This had been a hotel once, the Bristol Victoria. In its prime, it had been quite a hotel, its curb often crowded with chauffeured limousines. Now it was gone forever, and in its place would rise the new Stillman Towers.

Near the back of the lot, Jim saw a pair of feet sticking out from behind a stack of corrugated sheet metal that was leaning against the wall. He walked over and kicked the bottom of a foot.

"Come on, buddy, rise and shine. You need to get out of there," the equipment management specialist said. "I know you have to have some place to go, but this is dangerous."

Getting no response, Jim leaned down to look under the sheets of metal. "Hey," he said again, reaching up to grab the hand. "Come on, buddy, get out of—" He dropped the hand immediately. It was cold, stiff, and lifeless.

"He's dead!" Jim said, backing out and standing up. "He's *dead*! . . ."

BLACK OUT

LAW & ORDER

A novel by Jack Gregory
based on the Universal television series
LAW AND ORDER
created by
Dick Wolf

ST. MARTIN'S PAPERBACKS

Published by arrangement with MCA Publishing Rights, a Division of MCA Inc.

LAW AND ORDER: BLACK OUT

ISBN: 0-312-95009-8

Printed in the United States of America

St. Martin's Paperbacks edition/May 1993

10 9 8 7 6 5 4 3 2 1

Chapter One

Manhattan, Early Morning, September

Wisps of steam curled up from an underground vent, purpled, then dissipated in the gray light of early morning. Delivery trucks with clacking engines and grinding gears crept through the maze formed by other delivery trucks, which were stopped in the street. The parked trucks left room for passing traffic, though only for the most expert of drivers.

Traffic was particularly slow in one block of Fifty-first Street. Here, old buildings were being demolished and new construction was under way. As a result, large cranes, generators, and air compressors had become permanent fixtures, spilling out of the lot, across the sidewalk and into the street. In addition, a plank fence forced the pedestrians to leave the sidewalk and take a small walkway, which was itself constructed on the edge of the street, thus adding to the total congestion.

A large sign on the board fence identified the new project and the contractor. An architect's rendering of the building to be built on this site showed a huge slab towering into the sky, artfully shaped with inclined planes and intersecting lines, glistening with windows and a shining, black marble facade.

STILLMAN TOWERS, OFFICE SPACE NOW LEASING, the sign read. Beneath that was the name and telephone number of the agency handling the leasing. The construction contractor's name was also on the sign, as well as on the several pieces of equipment that remained on site during the construction. SANGREMANO CONSTRUCTION COMPANY.

Across the street from the construction site, on a billboard that spread across the third story of a neighboring building, was another sign:

AN APPEAL TO COMPASSION.
OVER 600 MEN, WOMEN, AND CHILDREN ARE BEING
MADE
HOMELESS BY THIS CONSTRUCTION! WHERE WILL THEY
GO?
STOP THE DESTRUCTION NOW!
FACE-IT.

A pickup truck with a sign on the door showing that it too belonged to Sangremano Construction, pulled to a stop. Its driver, Jim Siffer, was the first one on the site this morning, but then he always was. His job was to determine what new equipment would be needed today, if any, and how much longer the equipment which was already on site would have to remain before it could be taken elsewhere. Sangremano Construction had at least four other projects under way, and it was important that the equipment be utilized in the most efficient way.

Taking his clipboard with him, Jim began picking his way carefully through the rubble of the old building. This had been a hotel once, the Bristol Victoria. In its prime, the Bristol Victoria was quite a hotel, its curb often crowded with chauffeured limousines. Jim was fifty-five years old now, but he could remember once, when he was a child, seeing Humphrey Bogart coming through the front door. Jim had just seen *The Big Sleep*, and it was as if he were seeing part of the film come to life. Though not normally an autograph collector, Jim had gone up to Bogart and extended one of his schoolbooks sheepishly, asking for Bogart's autograph, explaining that this was the only paper he had.

Bogart laughed easily, then he pulled an envelope from his pocket, removed the letter, and signed the envelope.

"Here, kid," he said. "Use this." The return address on the envelope was Howard Hawks's, the director of *The Big Sleep*. Jim had long since lost the autograph, but he could still remember the day he got it.

Jim agreed with those who were protesting the destruction of the buildings, in that he had hated to see the old Bristol Victoria being torn down. But he disagreed with their reasons. They wanted the Bristol Victoria, and the other buildings also slated for destruction, to be converted into low-rent housing. Jim would have preferred to renovate the Bristol Victoria, preserving its own architecture and returning it to its original elegance. It was too late to think about that now. The Bristol Victoria was gone forever, and in its place would rise the new Stillman Towers.

There were some who sung the praises of the new architectural style, but Jim wasn't among their number. He thought most of the buildings today were sterile and without grace. He preferred the wedding-cake terraces and the gargoyles and cupolas of the older buildings. He sighed. Maybe that was why he was an equipment management specialist instead of an architect.

Near the back of the lot, Jim saw a pair of feet sticking out from behind a stack of corrugated sheet metal that was leaning against the wall. He walked over and kicked the bottom of a foot.

"Come on, buddy, rise and shine. You need to get out of there," he said. "I know you have to have some place to go, but this is dangerous. If a gust of wind was to blow this stuff down, you'd be crushed."

Getting no response, Jim leaned down to look under the leaning sheets of metal. Early morning shadows filled the little tunnel with darkness, so he couldn't see the face.

"Hey," he said again, reaching up to grab the hand. "Come on, buddy, get out of—" He dropped the hand immediately. It was cold, stiff, and lifeless.

"Son of a bitch!" Jim said, backing out and standing up. "Son of a bitch! He's dead!"

Quickly, Jim returned to the truck, then picked up the cellular phone.

When Phil Cerreta and Mike Logan arrived on the scene a little later that morning, they discovered not only the normally curious, but a well-organized group of demonstrators as well. The demonstrators were carrying signs demanding that the razing of the buildings be stopped. The name of the group, FACE-IT, was the same as on the huge billboard across the street.

Phil Cerreta, the older of the two men, was in his forties, stocky, with broad shoulders, a full chest, and a slight belly rise. He had dark, curly hair and a round face. Cerreta's younger partner, Mike Logan, was also dark-haired, but he was somewhat taller, slimmer, and with a longer face.

One of the demonstrators, a tall, thin, bearded young man, came toward the police car.

"How many more will they kill? How far will they go!" he shouted as the two officers got out of the car and hung their badge folders from their jacket pockets. "If they can't get the homeless out of here any other way, they murder them!"

"We're watching you, officers!" another shouted. "Don't you dare try to cover this up."

"Get back on the other side of the barricade," a uniformed cop growled to the demonstrators as he came over to lift the yellow crime scene tape for Cerreta and Logan.

"Who are these people?" Cerreta asked, nodding toward the demonstrators.

"Bunch of kooks," the uniform answered. "We've already had a dozen complaints on them before today. They've been stoppin' traffic and stickin' flyers in through the windows . . . botherin' the workers and the supply deliverers."

"They're FACE-IT," Logan said. "Haven't you read anything about them, or seen them on the news?"

"No," Cerreta replied.

"FACE-IT. That means 'Fair and Caring Enterprise, Immediate Tenancy.' They're into refurbishing old buildings for the homeless."

"Oh, yeah," Cerreta said. "I have heard something about that. What are they doin' here?"

"When the Bristol Victoria was torn down, it put a lot of people out into the street," the uniform said.

"What about our vic?" Cerreta asked. "Was he one of the homeless? Or one of them?" Again he nodded toward the demonstrators.

"*Justice . . . Justice . . . Justice!*" the demonstrators chanted.

"Homeless," the uniform said. "Only it isn't a he. It's a she."

"What?" Logan asked. "The call-in said male Cauc, between sixty and sixty-five."

"Yeah, well, that was before we had looked close," the uniform said. "Come on in—see for yourself."

Cerreta and Logan followed the policeman through a gate in the board fence that surrounded the construction site. Though separated from the street and the chanting demonstrators by no more than the thickness of the one-by-eight boards, the fence had the psychological effect of allowing them to pass from one world to another. Here was the world of the contractor: generators, air compressors, concrete mixers, ladders, scaffolds, wheelbarrows, and men. There were dozens of men standing around, most dressed in blue coveralls and yellow hard hats. One man, wearing, not blue coveralls, but a suit and an orange hard hat, came striding purposefully toward them. The front of his hat said Site Supervisor.

"You the two detectives we been waitin' on?" he asked.

"Who are you?" Logan replied.

"The name is Margolis—Paulie Margolis. I'm in charge of the men here. My question is, how long is this stiff goin' to have to lie around here before we can get back to work?"

"Your compassion for the victim is admirable," Logan said sarcastically. "I'm sure you'll be among the finalists in the humanitarian of the year award."

"Yeah? Don't give me that bullshit. I don't have the slightest bit of sympathy for her, or for any of these homeless bums. As far as I'm concerned they and those bleedin'-heart liberals carryin' the signs out there could all drop dead. They've been nothin' but a royal pain in the ass ever since we started work down here. Now, what about my question? When you goin' to get the stiff outta here so we can get back to work?"

"We'll have her out as quickly as we can," Cerreta replied. "In the meantime, sir, we thank you for your patience."

"Yeah, well, go ahead and do what you gotta do. Just don't be all day about it, okay? All these guys are gettin' paid for standin' around here, same as if they was workin'. Things like that can run you over budget pretty quick, and Mr. Sangremano doesn't like for his projects to run over budget."

"I'm sure he doesn't," Cerreta said as he and Logan started over toward the body. Another uniformed cop and a medical examiner were at the body. The examiner was squatting down for a closer look. Logan squatted beside the examiner.

"Jeez," Logan said. "They did in the whole side of the head. What could do that kind of damage?"

"The proverbial large blunt instrument," the M.E. answered. Then he shrugged. "I don't know . . . an iron pipe maybe, a rock, a brick. When I examine her, I can take a good look at the wound to see if there's any residue from the weapon."

"You didn't find anything here?" Cerreta asked the two uniformed cops.

"No, sir," one of them answered. "We've looked all over the place. We can't find anything that looks like it might have been used. 'Course, on a construction site like this, there's a thousand places something like that could be hidden."

"Then we need to look in a thousand places," Cerreta replied. "Anyone know who she is? Anyone ever seen her before?"

"Phil, have you seen enough?" the M.E. asked. "I'd like to get her back to Forensics for a closer look."

"We have pictures?"

"Plenty of them. Oh, and here are a couple of Polaroids for you two guys. Maybe they'll help you find someone to identify her."

Cerreta looked at the photos. The right side of the victim's face was covered with a cloth, blocking out the crushing and disfiguring wound.

"Not much of her face left to show," Cerreta said.

"Best we could do."

"I guess so. Yeah, go ahead, take her, see what you can find out in the exam."

"Okay, guys, let's get her out of here," the M.E. called to two of his assistants.

"Sergeant, those two guys over there say they've seen her around," one of the uniformed officers said, pointing toward a couple of the construction workers. Like the others, the two workers were just standing around, awaiting further directions.

"Thanks," Cerreta said, as he and Logan went over to talk to the two men.

The men identified themselves as Jerry Oliver

and Bud Melrose. Oliver was the older of the two.

"The officer over there said you two guys know her?" Cerreta asked.

Oliver shook his head. "No," he said. "We didn't say we knew her. We just said we'd seen her around."

"Where?"

"Here, at the site," Oliver replied. "She's been by here quite a few times. I've seen her lookin' in the trash for aluminum cans—that sort of thing."

"You don't have any idea where she lived, do you?"

"Where she lived? Hell, I thought she didn't live anywhere. I mean, isn't that what all the shoutin' is about? How there are so many homeless people and all?"

"Even the homeless tend to stay around a certain area," Logan said. "A doorway, an alley, a grate."

Oliver shook his head. "I don't know anything about that. All I know is I've seen her here before."

"And over at that place on Lexington—you know, the soup kitchen?" Melrose added. "I saw her standin' in line there the other day."

"Thanks," Cerreta said.

"Detective?" another worker said, walking up to join them. "That officer over there said I should speak with you two guys. My name is Jim Siffer. I'm the one who found her, this morning.''

''What time did you find her?''

''About six-thirty. I was here checking on the equipment we would need for today when I saw some feet sticking out from behind that sheeting over there. At first I thought it was just someone sleeping in here, so I tried to wake them up.''

''Is that fairly common?'' Logan asked. ''I mean, finding someone asleep here in the morning?''

Siffer shook his head. ''No, not really,'' he said. ''Every now and again you'll wake up someone who spent the night on the construction sight . . . but not that often.''

''Have you ever found anyone else on this particular site?''

Siffer shook his head again. ''No,'' he said. ''Actually, this isn't the kind of site they like to choose.''

''Why not?''

''There's no place for them. There's nothing here but smashed concrete and naked steel. None of the old building is still standing, there are no on-site construction shacks, so there's nowhere for them to find any shelter from the rain. Sometimes they'll sleep in the Dumpster, but even that's no good here. These Dumpsters are filled with bits of glass shards and rubble, all hard items, nothing in there that would provide them with warmth or a cushion. I have to admit I was a little surprised when I saw those legs sticking out from under there. Then, when I saw that he, uh, she, was dead, I called the police from the phone in my truck.''

The M.E.'s two assistants walked by them then, carrying the woman's rubber-sheeted body on a stretcher. They loaded it into the back of the M.E. van, then drove away.

"Hey!" Margolis shouted. "The stiff's gone now. Can I put these men back to work?''

"I'd appreciate it if you'd have them help us look for the murder weapon," Cerreta replied.

"What? Are you shittin' me? The city isn't paying their salary.''

"No, it isn't. But it is paying my partner and me, and we have to look for the murder weapon. It may take the two of us all day . . . if you get my drift.''

Margolis ran his hand through his hair, then sighed in disgust. "All right, all right," he said. "I'll have 'em look. What are they lookin' for?''

"Anything that might have been used to crush the victim's head in," Cerreta said. "If we're lucky, it'll have blood on it.''

* * *

They weren't lucky. After a thorough search of the site turned up nothing promising, Margolis, seething with anger and frustration, was told he could take his men back to work. Cerreta and Logan started back toward the car.

"I didn't expect to find anything here anyway," Cerreta said.

"You didn't?"

"No."

"Then why did we spend half the morning looking for it?"

"What we didn't find is as important as what we could have found," Cerreta said. "As far as I'm concerned, that pretty much proves that whoever killed her didn't kill her here."

"Yeah, I can go along with that," Logan said. "But I'll tell you what I can't figure out."

"What's that?"

"Who would want to kill her in the first place? I mean, what could they get out of it? She certainly didn't have anything anyone would want."

"The common denominator gets pretty low at times," Cerreta said. "She may have had a shawl. The nights are getting cold now. Someone could have killed her for as little as a blanket, or a hat, or a pair of gloves, no matter how ragged and full of holes they might be."

"Say, officer!" Melrose shouted, just as Cerreta and Logan reached the gate in the fence.

Both officers turned toward him. "Redemption House," Melrose said.

"Beg your pardon?"

"The soup kitchen where I saw the woman? I thought of the name of it. It's called Redemption House. You can't miss it—it's right over there on Lexington."

"Thank you," Cerreta said.

Redemption House, Noon

There were eight long tables in the big room, each flanked by backless wooden benches. There was nothing on any of the tables, no condiments, no napkins, no silverware of any kind. Along one wall and stretching all the way out into the street was a long line of derelicts, men and women. They trudged along slowly as those at the head of the line received their bowl of soup, a piece of bread, a cup of coffee, and a spoon, then joined those at the tables who were already eating.

There were two women standing out in the dining room watching the line, and two more behind the counter, serving. One of the women out front was wearing a crucifix. She was young, dark, slender, and very pretty. She walked over toward them.

"I'm Sister Theresa," she said. "Is there something I can do for you?"

"Yes, Sister, we're—" Cerreta started, reaching for his badge.

Smiling, Sister Theresa held up her hand to stop him. "You don't have to show me your badge. I know you're policemen. Plainclothes detectives would be my guess."

Logan smiled. "Your guess would be correct. You're very observant."

"Helping people is my avocation, observing them is my hobby. Now, you've something you want to ask?"

"Sister, I'm sorry to have to ask you to look at this, but . . ." Cerreta took the picture from his pocket and showed it to her. "Do you know this woman?"

Sister Theresa gasped, then crossed herself. "Bless the poor woman," she said. She pointed to the cloth. "I can't see all of her face."

"Believe me, Sister, you're seeing as much as you want," Logan said.

"Oh, I understand," Sister Theresa said quietly. She sighed. "I believe it's Mary."

"Mary? What's her last name?"

"Oh, I don't know her last name. Most of the poor creatures we get here have long ago abandoned their last names. Whether they do this out of embarrassment, or fear, or something else, we never know, nor do we ever pry."

"But you're sure this is the one you knew as Mary?"

"Oh yes, I'm quite sure."

"Sister, did you ever see her with anyone? We're looking for some way to get a more positive ID."

"She visited with us last night," Sister Theresa said. "Of course she was alone during the meal, though I did happen to notice her talking to someone out front, shortly after she had her supper."

"Do you know who she was talking to?" Cerreta asked. "Was it a man or a woman?"

"It was a man, and no, I don't believe I've ever seen him before. Actually, now that I think back on it, it looked more like they were arguing than talking. At the time, of course, I didn't think there was anything unusual about that."

"You didn't think there was anything unusual about them arguing? Why not?"

"You have to realize that Mary was quite different from our other guests," Sister Theresa said. "She was always a little standoffish. Of course, many of our people are shy . . . loners, you might say. But Mary took it a step further. She was . . . aloof."

"Aloof?"

"Yes. Aloof . . . almost regal."

"You mean she acted as if she were better than everyone else?"

"Yes, that's a good way of putting it. It sounds funny, doesn't it? Someone on skid row having such an attitude. But that was the way it was with Mary. Queen Mary, the others called her. Sometimes that difficulty in relating to the others resulted in rather vocal differences of opinion. I just assumed that was what I was seeing last night."

"Could you hear what Mary and the man were talking about?" Logan asked.

Sister Theresa shook her head. "No," she said. "I'm afraid not."

"What time did you observe this conversation?" Cerreta asked.

"Let me see. It was about seven o'clock, I think. Yes, I'm sure of it. Seven o'clock."

"And you've never seen the man before? The one she was talking to?"

"No."

"Did he look like a, uh—" Logan started, then stopped.

"Indigent," Cerreta supplied.

"No, now that I think of it, I don't believe he did."

"Could you describe him? Was he white or black? Old or young?"

"He was white, I'd say in his late forties or early fifties. I think I would recognize him again if I saw him," Sister Theresa said. "But as for giving a description . . ." She shrugged, then smiled. "I mean, I've seen shows on television where witnesses can describe a man so perfectly that police sketch artists can draw a picture of him. . . . I certainly don't think I could do that. All in all, he was rather unremarkable, I would say."

"How tall was he?" Logan asked.

"Oh, my, I don't have any idea."

"Smaller, about the same size, or taller than Mary?"

"Oh, yes, that would be a way to describe him, wouldn't it?" Sister Theresa replied. "He was about, oh, I would say, half a head taller than Mary."

"Did you notice the color of eyes or hair?"

"He was actually too far away from me to see the color of his eyes," Theresa said. "And he was wearing a hat. To be more specific, a sock cap."

"Thank you, Sister," Cerreta said. "You've been very helpful."

"Do you mind if we ask around?" Logan asked.

"No, go ahead, ask all the questions you wish," Sister Theresa said.

Separating, the two detectives asked everyone in the kitchen if they knew the woman in the photograph. Nearly a dozen identified her as Mary, some as "Queen" Mary, and one said he believed her name was Mary Mackie. No one ventured a thought as to who might have killed her, or why. Cerreta and Logan thanked them, then started to leave, when one of the men called out.

"Hey!"

"Yes?" Cerreta answered, turning toward him.

The man had long gray hair and a full, gray beard. He was wearing a sweater with several buttons missing, a flannel shirt, and a sock cap. He gripped his soup spoon in a hand that had long, dirty fingernails.

"What do you care?"

Cerreta took a step back toward him. "I beg your pardon?"

"About Mary?" the man said. "She was one of us." He made a circular motion with his soup spoon. "What do you care about one of us? You've got all those good citizens in the real world to take care of. Why are you wasting your time trying to determine who killed one of us?"

"Mary was a human being," Cerreta said. "Her life was as precious to her as any other human being's life is to them. Someone took that life from her. Whoever it was had no right to do that. I intend to find out who it was."

"You tryin' to tell us you really give a damn?"

"Yes, sir," Cerreta said. "I'm trying to tell you I really do give a damn."

The man took a spoonful of his soup, then held the spoon out toward Cerreta. "Look around the old Avery Building," he said. "I think she had a flop there."

Chapter Two

The Avery Building was surrounded by the same type of board fence that surrounded the construction site just next door. In addition, the doors and windows of the lower five floors were boarded shut. There were also several piles of trash on the ground in front between the board fence and the building. As Cerreta and Logan walked toward the boarded-up front entrance, a rat suddenly darted out from beneath one of the trash piles. Seeing the men, the rat stopped, looked at them with beady eyes and bared teeth, then turned and darted back into the pile.

"Jeez! Look at that!" Logan said.

Cerreta chuckled. "Are you surprised to see a rat here?"

"Yeah. No. I mean, I'm not surprised to see one, I just don't like the damn things." He stepped gingerly, carefully, around the next pile of trash. "With it all boarded up like this, I wonder how people get in and out."

"Like that," Cerreta said, pointing to the big piece of plywood over the front door. At that very moment, someone was pushing the edge out so they could exit the building.

"Excuse me, sir!" Cerreta called.

Startled, the man looked over toward them. Then, frightened, he pulled the plywood cover shut and disappeared back inside the building.

"What the hell did he run for?" Cerreta asked.

"He probably thinks we're here to kick him out," Logan replied.

When the two detectives reached the entrance, they pulled it open, then stepped inside. The lobby was a study of shadow and light. Scores of dust-mote-filled bars of sunlight stabbed down through gaps in the boarded-over windows. The light was not diffused. Rather, the sunbeams maintained their integrity, causing little circles and squares of light and shadow to spot the floor. The distant corners of the room were lost in darkness.

"Where did he go?" Logan asked.

"It doesn't really matter," Cerreta replied. "If he's in here, others are too. We'll just start trying the rooms until we find someone who can tell us where Mary lived.''

They climbed the stairs, then, when they came out onto the second-floor corridor, they were nearly overcome with the stench.

"Jesus! What is that?" Logan asked, coughing, and covering his nose with his handkerchief.

"If there's no electricity in here, what makes you think there would be plumbing?" Cerreta replied, covering his nose as well.

They found three of the rooms on the second floor occupied. When one of them finally realized that Cerreta and Logan weren't there to throw them out, she agreed to lead them to the room that had been Mary's.

"What's your name?" Cerreta asked.

"They call me Lucy," the woman said. She giggled. "Lucy Goosey."

"What would your real name be?"

"Lucille Ball."

"Lucille Ball? That's your real name?"

"Yeah, go figure. There were two of us. One of us got rich and famous. I'll let you decide which one," she said sarcastically.

They climbed six more flights of stairs, with the stench getting seemingly more powerful with each flight. But here at least there was more light, as the windows were only boarded up for the first five floors.

Lucy was a woman of an indeterminate age. She could have been in her fifties . . . or seventies. She was painfully thin, with prominent, almost skullish, cheekbones, and deep, sunken eyes.

"Queen Mary lived in there," she said, pointing to one of the doors.

"Do you know Mary's last name?"

"No."

"Weren't you and Mary friends?"

"We hardly ever had high tea together," Lucy said sarcastically.

"Who were her friends?"

"Queen Mary didn't have any friends."

"Surely, among all the people who live here, there was one person she was closer to than any other?" Cerreta insisted.

The woman shook her head again. "Queen Mary didn't want to be friends with the likes of us."

"With the likes of you? But she was one of you, wasn't she?" Logan asked.

"Not in her eyes, she wasn't. Queen Mary figured herself to be a cut above everyone else. You can ask the others if you want. But you'll find that I'm tellin' the truth. She didn't have any friends because she didn't want any friends."

Logan tried the door and it opened easily. He and Cerreta stepped in.

"You need me anymore?" their guide asked.

"Just one more question," Cerreta said. "When is the last time you saw her?"

"I saw her at eight o'clock last night," Lucy said.

"Where did you see her?"

"Down on the street, near where the old hotel was before they tore it down."

"Eight o'clock. Are you sure of the time?"

"Well, my Rolex is out for repairs," Lucy said dryly. "But it was eight o'clock when I left Charlie's, and that was just a few minutes before."

"Who is Charlie?"

"Charlie isn't a who, it's a what," Lucy said. "It's a liquor store up on Fifty-third."

"We'll be wanting to get a statement from you, Miss Ball. Don't go away," Cerreta said.

"You're in luck," Lucy said. "I've decided against going to Florida this year. I'll be here. That is, until they tear the building down and run me off."

After Lucy left, Logan said, "Look at this room, would you, Phil? It's like finding a rose in a cabbage patch."

"I'll be . . ." Cerreta whistled softly. "Who would have thought this?"

All the other rooms they had seen in the building had been filthy hovels, furnished, if at all, with no more than a pile of rags for a bed, or at best, a salvaged mattress. This room wasn't like that. To begin with, it was impeccably clean. And it had a real bed, which was neatly made, complete with a bedspread. There was also a dresser, a table, and a chair.

Logan started opening the dresser drawers. "Here's something," he said, taking out a large brown envelope. Opening the envelope, he found a framed, eight-by-ten black-and-white photo.

"What is it?" Cerreta asked.

"Some young woman on a horse," Logan replied, showing it to Cerreta. "I don't have any idea who it is."

"My guess is it's Mary."

"Can't be. This girl's not over twenty or twenty-one."

"Look at that car," Cerreta said. "That's a 'fifty-nine Chrysler Imperial. This photo is over thirty years old. When we get the computer people to compare this picture with what we've got, I think you'll find it's the same person."

"If it is, maybe they can age this picture so we have something better to go on than what we have now," Logan suggested.

"Good idea," Cerreta agreed. He looked around the room. "I tell you what, before we touch anything else in here, let's get the lab boys down to dust for prints. According to everything we've heard, Mary had no friends. I'm going to be interested to see if there are any prints in here besides hers.''

Forensic Lab

"Hi," Logan said, stepping into the M.E.'s office. "What have you got for us?''

"Nothing yet," the M.E. replied. "I'm just about to get into it.''

"Jeez, you haven't even done the examination yet?''

"I had two ahead of her," the M.E. said. "Besides, she didn't mind waiting," he added with a laugh.

"Very funny."

"Come along, I'll let you watch.''

"That's not my idea of a fun afternoon.''

"Maybe not, but you'll get the report faster.''

Logan sighed. "All right, all right, I'll be your audience.''

"Good, I'm always much better before an audience," the M.E. quipped. "Get into scrubs.''

A moment later both Logan and the M.E. were in scrubs and mask. In addition, the M.E. was wearing rubber gloves. He completed his preparation by clipping on a small microphone so he could record his findings. After that he walked back into the lab, with Logan reluctantly following close behind.

The victim's body was lying on the table, totally naked, bluish gray in color. She was a small woman, and she looked even smaller in death. Her breasts were barely discernible, and her rib cage was boldly defined. Her body recessed deeply just below the rib cage, and her hipbones were prominent. Though the hair on her head was gray, her pubic hair was very dark, a startling contrast to the otherwise colorless display.

The M.E. began talking into the tape recorder. "Okay, here we go. It's three-fifteen P.M., September twenty-second. I am Dr. Henry Baker, medical examiner in and for the City of New York, duly constituted and commissioned to disturb the corpse in the course of my examination. This examination is being witnessed by Detective Mike Logan of the New York police. The body is that of an unknown Caucasian female, approximately . . . oh, I'd say, fifty-five to sixty years old. The right side of the face is distorted because of an irregular deforming wound that involves the lateral aspect of the orbit, brow, and the right maxilla. A large amount of dried blood is present on the skin surface, and the wound is an extremely irregular defect that completely obliterates the eyes, lids, and extends from the extreme right forehead to the level of the nasolabial fold. The cavity of the frontal sinus can be seen through the opening of the wound. I am taking samples from the wound to examine any foreign matter which may have come from the instrument which caused the wound."

Dr. Baker scraped parts of the dried blood and tissue from several different places around the wound onto a cotton gauze pad. Then, carefully, he put the pad into a small box.

"There is one wound over the anterolateral aspect of the right breast that is approximately eight centimeters in greatest dimension. I am taking samples from this wound to examine any foreign matter which may have come from the instrument which caused the wound."

Again Dr. Baker made scrapings onto a cotton gauze pad, putting that sample into a separate box. He moved down her body to the abdomen to resume his examination.

"I am taking samples from both the vagina and the rectum to determine the presence of sperm. I will also take samples of debris from the inner aspect of the thighs as well as fingernail scrapings from under the nails of both hands and samples of pubic and scalp hair.

"Do you think she was raped?" Logan asked.

"There's no way of determining that," Dr. Baker said. "I couldn't even tell you if she had sex unless the male ejaculated."

Dr. Baker put the samples he spoke of into

small vials, then he put the vials on the porcelain table alongside the small boxes containing the gauze pads. After that he took out his camera and began taking pictures. He placed a ruler near the cuts and bruises in order to measure the size of the wounds. Finally he finished his examination and he draped a sheet over the body.

"She has wonderful bone structure," the doctor said. "She must've been a beautiful woman at one time."

Logan thought of the picture of the young woman on horseback. "If the picture I saw today was her . . . she was," he said.

Dr. Baker looked up in surprise. "You've identified her?"

"Not yet. But we found a photograph in her room that we think is of her as a younger woman. That's a step in the right direction."

Construction Site on Fifty-first

The group of FACE-IT demonstrators had varied in size throughout the day. It had been at its largest just after the woman's body was discovered that morning. Then, they had been able to take advantage of the TV cameras and newspaper reporters. A couple of times they even managed to get one of the reporters to come over and talk to them, and to take pictures.

For a while they were kept going by the excitement of knowing that the cause they were so ardently representing was going to be on the news. As the day wore on, however, the newspaper and TV reporters left. Then the curiosity seekers quit coming around, and even the traffic on the street ignored them. Without the excitement to stimulate them, the number of demonstrators gradually grew smaller. By three-thirty in the afternoon there were only four demonstrators left, and they may as well not have even been there, for all the attention they were getting.

It was, perhaps, that lack of attention that spurred them into action. Under the urging of one of their group, all four crossed the street, then went in through the gate in the fence and out onto the construction site. At that point the bearded leader of the group, seeing an open can of red paint, seized it and ran toward a group of construction workers who had not yet noticed them.

"Behold the Angel of Death!" he shouted, splashing the startled workers, and himself, with red paint.

Station House

"How did the medical exam go?" Cerreta asked when Logan returned sometime later.

"She was killed by the blow to the head. He's still looking for residue that might identify the instrument that was used."

"What did he find?"

"Traces of ferrous oxide, which means it could have been anything from an iron pipe to a hammer."

"Or it could mean that flakes of rust fell down onto the wound from the corrugated metal she was found under."

"Possible, but not probable," Logan said. "The rust was embedded into her wound, as if it had been driven in. In addition to the rust, there was some dirt, some cotton fiber, some lye, and a trace of turpentine."

"Lye?"

"Dr. Baker thinks it may be from lye soap."

"What about the turpentine? Anything significant there?"

"I don't know. Wouldn't painters use it to clean their brushes or something? I'm sure there's turpentine around a construction site, somewhere," Logan said.

"There's no painting going on yet," Cerreta

pointed out. "Maybe if we could find where they are painting, we could get a lead."

Logan shook his head. "I don't know," he replied. "I don't think so. There wasn't all that much turpentine. There was just a trace. He also checked to see if there'd been any recent sexual activity."

"Had there been?"

"He found no trace of male ejaculation," Logan said. "What have you found out?"

"You remember one of the men said he thought her name was Mary Mackie?"

"Yeah. Anything there?"

"If she is a Mackie, she's not a New York Mackie," Cerreta said. "I've checked with every Mackie family in the book—no one has any missing relatives."

"What about the computer people? Have they matched the photo?"

"Yes, well, we do get a break there," Cerreta said. "There's a ninety percent chance the picture of the girl on the horse is of Mary as a young woman."

"Ninety percent?"

"What do you want? That's pretty good."

"I'd like a hundred percent."

"Yeah, I'm sure the D.A. would too. Under the circumstances, though, ninety is all we're going to get."

"What about the aging?"

"They haven't finished."

"Do they still have the photo?"

"No, they've scanned it into the program already," Cerreta said. He pulled open his desk drawer. "We've got the photo back."

Logan took it from him and studied it for a moment. He felt unusually drawn to the photograph. There was something about her, about the expression on her face, the look in her eyes, her posture on the horse. She was dressed in a riding habit, holding the reins with her left hand and a small riding quirt in her right. Her mouth was fixed into a slight, provocative smile, as if she were being coy with the photographer. That provocativeness came across in the photograph, bridging the years and connecting with Logan in a way that he found almost disturbing.

"Dr. Baker is right," he said quietly.

"I beg your pardon?"

"She was a beautiful woman."

"You think so?" Cerreta asked.

"Of course," Logan replied, almost defensively. "Don't you?"

Cerreta looked at her. "I don't know. I guess I like them a bit more . . . earthy."

"Earthy?" Logan laughed.

"Approachable," Cerreta said. "This looks like Grace Kelly . . . I prefer Sophia Loren."

"That's just your ethnic bias getting the better of—'' Logan suddenly snapped his fingers. ''By damn, you're right!'' he said.

''You mean you agree with me?''

''Yes! At least the part about her being like Grace Kelly. What do you think of when you think of Grace Kelly?''

''She was pretty, she was a princess.''

''Even before that—in her movies—wasn't there sort of a cool elegance to her? A regal beauty? An aloofness? Like a beautiful, wealthy, socialite?''

''I'd say that describes her,'' Cerreta agreed.

''And it describes Mary too,'' Logan said. ''You heard what that nun said. And the woman in the building. They both said that Mary was standoffish and aloof. And look at this picture. If this isn't the photograph of a wealthy young socialite, I'll eat my badge.''

Cerreta, seeing a civilian with a visitor's pass wandering around, held up his hand to stop Logan from saying anything else.

''Yes, sir, can I help you?'' he asked.

''I'm looking for Captain Cragen?''

''He's in the office at the rear. Just knock on the door,'' Cerreta said.

''Thank you,'' the civilian said.

''Phil, what do you think about giving this picture to the TV and newspapers? Maybe someone will recognize her,'' Logan suggested.

''I don't know. For every one who might recognize her, we'll have one hundred who claim to. If we have to, we'll do it . . . but I'm not ready for that yet."

The phone on Cerreta's desk buzzed and he picked it up.

"Cerreta."

"Phil, why don't you and Mike come on into my office? I have someone I want you to meet," Captain Cragen said.

"Be right there," Cerreta said. As he hung the phone up, he looked at Logan. "The captain wants us to meet the civilian who just came in."

Captain Cragen, tall, thin, and balding, was leaning back in his chair as Cerreta and Logan came in. He was holding a fountain pen in one hand, tapping it lightly against the other, then he leaned forward and put his arms on the desk.

"Gentleman, this is Hence Fielding," Cragen said. "Mr. Fielding, these are the two officers who are working the case. Detective Sergeant Cerreta and Detective Logan."

"Gentlemen," Fielding said, standing and offering his hand. Cerreta took it. Logan, who had come no farther in than the file cabinet, just nodded.

"You have some information on the case, Mr. Fielding?" Cerreta asked.

"I'm afraid not," Fielding replied.

"Then I don't understand. What's your interest in the case?"

Fielding turned toward Captain Cragen. "Perhaps the captain can explain my offer to you."

"Your offer?"

"Mr. Fielding has offered to put up a fifty thousand dollar reward for any information that will lead to the apprehension and conviction of the murderer," Cragen said.

"Mr. Fielding, did you *know* the victim?" Logan asked.

"Uh, no, not exactly."

"What does that mean, not exactly?"

"It means that I didn't know her personally. However, she was one of my people."

"One of your people?"

"Mr. Fielding is the founder of FACE-IT," Cragen explained.

"You mean that bunch of kooks carrying the signs?" Cerreta asked.

"They are not kooks, Sergeant Cerreta," Fielding said. "They are good and conscientious people, dedicated to stopping the destruction of renewable living space. It's too late to do anything about the Bristol Victoria, it has already been destroyed. But it isn't too late to stop the destruction of the Avery Building. That's the only home those poor people have."

"Mr. Fielding, I don't know what you call 'home,' but have you been in the Avery Building lately?'' Cerreta asked. ''To say nothing of the fact that it has been closed, condemned, and is dangerous . . . it is also a pigsty, and a breeding place for rats. There is no electricity, no water or sewage. The stairways and halls smell like toilets—which they are—and every corner is a mugging, or murder, waiting to happen.''

Fielding smiled, a beneficent smile. ''Yes, isn't it? And so was Pierpont Place before the renovation. Now, I'm happy to say, it is filled with happy and productive people who own their own homes.''

''Pierpont Place?''

''A building, not unlike the Bristol Victoria,'' Fielding said. ''Long ago abandoned, and in arrears for taxes, it had been taken over by the city and was slated for demolition. It made no difference that the building was occupied by several people who had no other place to go. The cold, unfeeling bureaucracy of city government said it was coming down, and that was that. Scores of people were going to be thrown into the cold, with no provisions for their survival.

''I read about it in the paper and, becoming concerned about the fate of those poor unfortunate people, decided to do something about it. I managed to secure a court order delaying the demolition, then I convinced the city to turn the deed over to FACE-IT. In the meantime, the poor people in the area went to work. They completely refurbished the building, reconnected sewer and electricity, and moved in. I then arranged for a series of Title 8 loans, and now Pierpont Place is occupied by productive homeowners with an investment in their own neighborhood.''

''And you see something like that for the Avery Building?'' Logan asked.

''I do indeed, sir. I do indeed,'' Fielding said. ''Don't you agree?''

''No,'' Logan said. ''The Pierpont Building was city property—converting it to low-cost housing was a practical solution. But the Bristol Victoria and the Avery Building belong to Stillman Properties. That's a private company, and if they want to tear down old, condemned buildings and replace them with new structures, that's their right.''

Fielding clucked his tongue and shook his head. ''Spoken like a true defender of the capitalist system,'' he said. ''You have a passion for the letter of the law, sir, but no compassion for the people who are subject to those laws. Ah, but perhaps we can agree on one thing? Whoever committed the foul deed against this poor, homeless creature, must be found, and made to pay the fullest penalty the law will allow.''

''Yes,'' Logan replied. ''We can agree on that.''

"Good, then you won't mind if I offer a fifty thousand dollar reward for any information that will help you in your job."

"That's up to you, Mr. Fielding. I'm afraid we have nothing to do with that end of it."

"Yes, I know. But not to worry. I shall make all the necessary arrangements."

"We'll see you out," Cerreta offered.

"I see. You find my presence disturbing, do you?" Fielding smiled. "Don't worry, Sergeant, we are not adversaries. However, if you wish to show me out, I will welcome it as a friendly gesture."

As the three walked by the desk sergeant's desk a moment later, they saw two uniformed policemen with four prisoners in custody. Cerreta recognized one of the prisoners as the bearded young man who had confronted him earlier in the day. He was easy to pick out because he was splashed with red.

"What is that?" Cerreta asked, pointing to the red prisoner. "That isn't blood."

"Yes, it is blood!" the prisoner shouted. "It's the blood of the innocent, spilled by an indifferent society!"

"It's paint," one of the uniforms said disgustedly. "These guys came onto the construction site a while ago, and this one threw a gallon of red paint onto the workers."

"What was the idea of that?"

"The paint is the visual symbol for the blood they have on their hands. They are responsible for that poor woman's death."

Cerreta shook his head, then looked over at Fielding. "Are these your people?" he asked.

The prisoner in red had not noticed Fielding until that moment. "Mr. Fielding! Mr. Fielding, I'm Bertis Grisham. You remember me, don't you? Bertis Grisham? I demonstrated for you in front of the Pierpont Building, remember?"

"Yes, Mr. Grisham, I do remember you," Fielding said.

"You understand what we did, don't you?"

"Yes, of course," Fielding said. "And don't worry, I'll see to it that your bail is made."

"Bless you, Mr. Fielding," Grisham said. "Bless you."

"You approve of that?" Cerreta asked, as they walked away from the group.

"In principle, yes," Fielding replied. "After all, I think history has proven that civil disobedience can be a powerful—and honorable—weapon to use when it is used to seek justice."

"And you think throwing a can of paint on construction workers is an honorable way to seek justice?" Cerreta asked.

Fielding chuckled. "When you consider that Mr. Grisham once suggested that the best way to bring the demolition to a halt would be to commit ritualistic suicide . . . I think his alternative is quite preferable."

When Cerreta and Logan returned to their desks, there was a message waiting, asking one of them to call the lab. Logan made the call.

"Yeah, this is Logan," he said when his call was answered.

"This is Cookson. I've got a fingerprint match for you from the victim's room."

"Hey, good work," Logan said. "I have to hand it to you—it didn't take you very long."

"What can I say?" Cookson replied. "Sometimes when you're playing center field, the ball just falls in your glove. You know what I mean?"

"No, I can't say as I do," Logan replied.

"I'd just finished working the prints from the room. We've got six good sets, and one of them I just saw again, right in front of me."

"Where?"

"One of that bunch of demonstrators they brought in today. They printed them—routine —and there it was. The prints in the victim's room belong to Bertis Grisham."

"Thanks, Cookson," Logan said. "I owe you one." He hung up the phone and smiled broadly at Cerreta. "We have a match on the prints in Mary's room."

Chapter
Three

"**H**ere's Grisham's rap sheet," Logan said, dropping a couple of pages on the desk in front of Cerreta.

"It's pretty long," Cerreta replied, picking it up.

"Yeah, but it's all petty stuff: trespassing, blocking traffic, public nuisance, that type thing. He's a joiner . . . before FACE-IT he was involved with the Environmental Battle Group." Logan chuckled. "He and several others once let the air out of the tires of an entire fleet of vehicles belonging to a company that had been cited for its smoke emissions polluting the air. They said the air in the tires would 'symbolically' replace the polluted air."

"Big on symbolic action, isn't he?"

"Hello, what's this?" Logan said. "Here's one that's a little more than symbolism. Amalgatech Industries was doing business in South Africa. One of the causes Grisham was involved with was protesting such companies. To make his point, Grisham detonated a bomb in the Amalgatech rest room. According to this, the bomb was set to go off when no one was there, but it just missed killing a night employee who'd left the facilities moments before the blast.

"And how about this?" Cerreta replied. "He also beat up an employee of a company that used chimpanzees in medical research." Cerreta looked up. "The employee he beat up was a woman."

"What do you say we talk to Mr. Grisham?" Logan suggested.

Interrogation Room A

Bertis Grisham was a thin-faced, hawk-nosed young man, with dark brown eyes that shined with intensity. He wore his ash-blond hair medium long and combed straight back, without a part. There were red blotches on his skin—not from paint residue, but from the effort of cleaning the paint off. The lawyer with him was small and bald, except for a line of hair above each ear. He was wearing dark-rimmed glasses.

"My name is William Barkett. Mr. Fielding hired me to represent Mr. Grisham and the other gentlemen who were brought in this afternoon. I would like it to be noted that we are prepared to cooperate fully with your interrogation, though I wonder why you asked only Mr. Grisham and not the others, since they were all charged equally."

"Mr. Barkett, we aren't interested in the paint-throwing episode," Cerreta replied. "I'm Detective Sergeant Phil Cerreta, this is Detective Mike Logan. We're with Homicide, and we'd like to ask your client a few questions about the woman who was found murdered on the construction site this morning."

"Wait a minute, hold it," Barkett said, holding out his hands. "I was hired to represent defendants who are being charged with malicious disturbance of the peace. Are you now saying that he is being charged with murder?"

"Not at the moment, counselor, but your client has been present on the scene for many days," Cerreta replied. "He may have some information that is relevant to the case."

Barkett stroked his chin for a moment, then he nodded. "I don't know about this," he said. He looked at Grisham. "Mr. Grisham, you may want to hire your own attorney for this."

"I can't afford a lawyer," Grisham said. "But I have nothing to hide. I welcome the questions." He looked around the room. "Where's the press?"

"I beg your pardon?"

"The press," Grisham repeated. "I want full press coverage of this conference."

"This isn't a press conference, Mr. Grisham," Logan said. "This is an interrogation."

"An interrogation, or an inquisition?" Grisham said. "Who's paying your salary? Sangremano? Stillman? The military-industrial complex? The Tri-Patriot Commission?"

"Why, you're paying our salary, Mr. Grisham," Cerreta said easily. "We're employed by the taxpaying citizens of New York."

"You understand, do you not, that you have the right to refuse to answer our questions," Logan said.

"My advice to you at this point, Mr. Grisham, is to not answer any of the questions until you have a lawyer who is prepared to represent you should this go any further," Barkett said.

"I told you, I can't afford a lawyer."

"One will be appointed for you," Barkett said, "as I'm sure these gentlemen are about to point out."

"That is correct," Logan said. "If you desire a lawyer and cannot afford one, one will be appointed."

"I don't want a lawyer. Ask away."

"Mr. Barkett, are you going to represent him?"

Barkett sighed. "Mr. Fielding hired me to represent him. I shall continue to do so until I am told otherwise. I will advise him during this interrogation. But again, Mr. Grisham, my advice is to refuse to answer."

"Refuse to answer? Why should I refuse?" Grisham asked. "Unlike certain members of our government, I am responsible for my actions. Each and every action that I take is for a calculated reason . . . and I will gladly share that reason with you."

"Did you kill the woman who was found on the construction site this morning?" Logan asked.

"What kind of question is that?" Barkett said sharply. "I thought you were only going to ask him questions about anything he might know that is relevant to the case."

Logan laughed. "What could be more relevant, counselor?" he asked.

"I thought you were questioning Mr. Grisham as a witness. Are you now saying he is a suspect?"

"Yes."

"What possible leap of logic would cause you to suspect him?"

"Mr. Grisham is an activist who has, in the

past, gone to extremes to call attention to a particular cause," Cerreta said.

"I know of Mr. Grisham's history of activism," Barkett said. "He is a conscientious man, intensely dedicated to what he believes in. I think he should be admired for that, not ostracized, and certainly not made a suspect for a murder."

"Mr. Grisham, did you or did you not once make the comment that something like a ritualistic suicide would bring enough public attention onto a demolition project to cause the demolition to be stopped?" Cerreta asked.

"Don't answer that question," Barkett ordered.

"Why shouldn't I answer it?" Grisham replied. He smiled. "Yes, I did make that statement," he said. "And I was quite willing to make the gesture if it took it."

"The gesture, or the deed?" Logan asked.

Grisham chuckled. "You don't get it, do you? You just don't get it. The deed *is* the gesture, and the gesture *is* the deed."

"Did you kill that woman?" Logan asked again.

"Why would I want to kill her? Don't you understand what I am about? I've devoted my entire life to helping others. That poor creature who was killed is one of the very ones I'm trying to save. Anyway, why are you asking me such questions? Why don't you ask Luigi Sangremano? He's the destroyer here. He's the one who crushes lives as easily as he crushes buildings.''

"And you wouldn't hurt a fly, right, Grisham?" Cerreta asked.

"Someone like you—living your life on the edge of violence as you do—might find it difficult to understand compassion, true compassion," Grisham said. "But try."

"Was it compassion that led you to set off the bomb in the rest room of Amalgatech Industries?"

"It was set to go off in the middle of the night so as not to kill or maim, but merely to send a message. No one was hurt . . . except for the poor South African blacks whose spirits were being crushed by Amalgatech's policies," Grisham said. "Amalgatech was doing business with the white masters in South Africa, enriching the company and their stockholders on the blood of innocents."

"Speaking of innocents, what about the night watchman who just missed being killed by your bomb? He had just used the rest room a moment earlier. It was only by the grace of God that no one was hurt," Cerreta said.

"The point is, he wasn't hurt. Anyway, in any battle there are risks," Grisham replied. "The idea is to minimize the risks and maximize the gains."

"Who took the risks when you beat up Emily Pierce?" Logan growled.

"*I* took the risks," Grisham said, smiling and holding up his finger.

"You took the risks? That's a funny way of looking at it," Cerreta said.

"It's the only way of looking at it," Grisham replied. "After all, I served six months in prison. The only indignity Miss Pierce suffered was a black eye and a cut lip."

"Tell me, what noble purpose did you serve by beating up a woman?"

"It was symbolic. Like the paint today."

"You're great on symbolism, aren't you, Mr. Grisham?"

"Yes. It's no accident that the only message left to us by our cave-dwelling ancestors are symbols. Symbolism is the most powerful form of communication there is."

"What's symbolic about beating up a woman?"

"Miss Pierce was an employee of Biotesting Inc., a company that tested toxic chemicals on helpless chimpanzees—not for medicine, mind you, not to find a cure for AIDS, or cancer, or heart disease, or even the common cold. No, their research consists solely of testing such things as lipstick, face powder, and hair spray to determine what ingredients are poison and what ingredients are safe for the painted face. The folly of women's vanity is all the excuse they need to torture those poor, helpless creatures. It was only fitting, then, that a woman be chosen for my retribution. As the chimpanzees were helpless before her, she was helpless before me. That, sir, was the symbolism."

"Did you kill the woman whose body was found on the construction site?" Cerreta asked again.

"Detective, you've already asked that question, and Mr. Grisham has answered it," Barkett said.

"He evaded the answer," Cerreta said.

"Did I? Then I'll answer it for you now. No, I did not kill that woman," Grisham said.

"Do you have some reason for asking these questions?" Barkett asked. "Or are you merely on a fishing expedition?"

"We have a reason," Logan said.

"I'd like to hear it."

"Yes, so would I," Grisham said.

"Mr. Grisham, we found your fingerprints in the victim's room."

"That's enough!" Barkett suddenly said. "Mr. Grisham, now I must insist that you answer no more questions."

"But I want to answer the question," Grisham said. He smiled at Cerreta and Logan. "You see, officers, I am not merely a benign demonstrator, carrying signs to be seen by others. My involvement with these people—my love for them —goes far beyond that. I've often taken them food, medicine, blankets, and clothing. Those missions of mercy have taken me into every room in the Avery House, and the Bristol Victoria before it was demolished. I have no doubt that my fingerprints are all over the place. I certainly hope so, anyway."

"We'll be checking on that, Mr. Grisham," Logan said.

"Please do. Oh, and you might also check where I was between four-thirty yesterday afternoon and six o'clock this morning."

"Oh? And where were you between eight o'clock last night and eight o'clock this morning?"

Grisham laughed dryly. "I was in jail," he said. "Isn't that the sweetest irony? You're trying to make a case against me, but you can't, because I was in your jail."

"Did you throw paint yesterday too?" Logan growled disgustedly.

"Nothing quite so glamorous," Grisham replied. "My only offense yesterday was to disrupt traffic. New York's finest picked three of us up at a little after eight last night. If you don't believe me, check with the Eighteenth Precinct."

Logan leaned back in his chair and crossed his arms on his chest.

Cerreta stroked his chin, then made an impatient motion with his hand. "All right," he said with a sigh. "Get out of here."

"Gentlemen, I hold no ill will toward you," Grisham said as he stood. "I know you're merely trying to do your job, and believe me, I'm on your side. I too want the murderer apprehended. As I said, I have love and compassion for these people. I do have one thing that you might find helpful."

"What is that?"

"Peter Sondheim."

"Who?"

Grisham smiled and held his finger up knowingly. "Peter Sondheim," he said. "Check it out."

Police Station House, the Next Morning

"Peter Sondheim was killed two years ago," Logan said.

"Same kind of case?"

"Not exactly. That is, he wasn't an indigent like Mary was. But he *was* killed on a construction site."

"Interesting," Cerreta said.

"Prosecution tried to make the case that Luigi Sangremano ordered the man killed but one of Sangremano's lieutenants took the fall."

"That's loyalty for you," Cerreta said.

"Yeah, well, he got paid well for it. The word is, Sangremano settled half a million dollars on the lieutenant's family to see them through the difficult 'times."

Cerreta stood up and reached for his jacket. "What do you say you and I pay Mr. Sangremano a visit?" he suggested, slipping the jacket on over his shoulder holster.

Sangremano Construction Company, Eighteenth and Tenth

A chain-link fence closed off the lot so that access could be gained only through a gate. When Logan turned toward the gate, a security guard came out from the little shack to meet the car. Logan rolled the window down.

"What can I do you for?" the security guard asked.

Logan flashed his badge. "We're here to speak with Luigi Sangremano."

"Does Mr. Sangremano know you're coming?"

"We didn't come here to 'do lunch' with him," Logan growled. "This is police business. Now open the gate."

"Yes, sir," the guard said, walking back to his shack and pressing the button that opened the gate. As Logan started through, however, he saw the security guard pick up the telephone.

The lot was busy with forklifts, cranes, and generators, as well as large and small trucks being loaded or unloaded with construction equipment and materials. Logan parked in one of the empty reserved parking spots right in front of the door of the building marked "Office." Inside, an attractive young woman was sitting at a desk. She was just hanging up the phone when they came in, and she looked up nervously.

"Is there something I can do for you gentlemen?" she asked.

"I'm sure the security guard told you who we were," Cerreta said.

The young woman bit her lip and looked at the phone. "Uh, yes, sir, he said you were policemen," she admitted.

"Good. That saves a lot of time. We're here to see Mr. Sangremano."

"I'm afraid Mr. Sangremano is going to be tied up with meetings all morning," she said.

"That's all right, we'll only take a minute,"

Cerreta said, starting toward a door in the back of the room.

"Just a minute, sir! You can't go in there!" the woman called.

Ignoring her, Cerreta opened the door. Then, only when it was open, he knocked on it. Luigi Sangremano, short, stocky, with a round face and a crop of black hair, was sitting behind his desk, smoking a cigar. There were two other men in the office with him, standing near the desk. The three of them were looking at papers spread out on the desk.

"Who the hell are you?" Sangremano asked sharply. "What are you doing coming in here like this?"

"I'm sorry, Mr. Sangremano," the reception-ist said, standing in the doorway, behind the plainclothesmen. "I tried to stop them but they barged right on in."

"We're police officers, Mr. Sangremano," Cerreta said, showing his badge. "We'd like to talk to you about the body that was found on one of your construction sites yesterday."

"That's all right, Darlene," Sangremano said, waving his hand to dismiss her concern. "I'll talk to them." Then to Logan and Cerreta, "You couldn't of had the courtesy to call ahead so I could maybe plan my schedule?"

"We won't take too much of your time, Mr. Sangremano," Cerreta promised.

"Yeah, well, all right, I'll talk to you. Let's see, that happened over at the Bristol Victoria, didn't it?"

"Yes."

"Oh, these are a couple of my associates . . . Tony Villipianni and John Conti."

"Tony Villipianni? I thought you were serving time for murder," Logan said. Villipianni was the name of the lieutenant who had taken the fall for killing Peter Sondheim.

"It wasn't murder, it was Manslaughter Two," Villipianni corrected. "And I've been out for almost six months."

"It was a weak case to begin with," Sangremano said easily. "Listen, Tony, John, how 'bout you take care of those things we talked about this morning while I entertain these officers?"

"Sure thing, Mr. Sangremano," Villipianni said as he and Conti left.

"Sit down, gentlemen, sit down," Sangremano offered in a grand gesture. He pointed toward a silver case on his desk. "Would either of you care for a cigar?"

"No, thank you," Cerreta said, declining the cigar, though he and Logan did sit.

"No? Well, if you'll excuse me, mine needs a relight," Sangremano said. He picked up an oversized lighter, snapped it, then held the flame to the end of his cigar. He puffed, sucking in his cheeks and creating a cloud of blue smoke. "So," he finally said. "Let's talk."

"Before we do, I think it might be wise for us to tell you your rights."

"Why do you need to do that? Am I bein' charged with something?" Sangremano asked, raising his eyebrows in surprise.

"No, but we'll be asking specific questions. I think it's better all around if we go through the proper procedure."

"Yeah, sure, if it makes you feel better, go ahead," Sangremano said, waving his hand almost distractedly.

"You have the right to remain silent. You have the right to an attorney. If you want one and cannot afford one, an attorney will be provided for you. Do you understand these rights?"

"Yeah, yeah." Sangremano chuckled. "If I can't afford one," he snorted. "I got three of the sonsofbitches on retainer."

"Do you want to call one now? If so, we'll wait until he arrives before we begin our discussion."

"No, no, go ahead. I got nothin' to hide," Sangremano said. "By the way, what was the name of the woman who was killed, anyway?"

"Mary."

"Mary? That's all you have? Mary? No last name?"

"That's all we know."

"That's a shame," Sangremano said. "When a person dies, someone should at least know their last name. Otherwise, it's like they never were here at all, you know what I mean? Who was she, anyway? One of the indigents?"

"Yes. Are they causing you much trouble?"

"The indigents? No, not really," Sangremano said, shaking his head. "No, the ones causing me trouble are that bunch of kooky do-good bastards who are out there picketing every day. I've complained to the cops about them half a dozen times, but they're still there. Why the hell won't the police do anything about it?"

"A little thing called freedom of speech," Logan said. "They have every right to picket and protest . . . guaranteed by the Constitution."

"Yeah? Do they have the right to come onto the property and do damage? Like yesterday, for example. I understand a bunch of those sonsofbitches came in and threw red paint all over my men. Is that free speech too?"

"No, sir, that goes beyond free speech," Cerreta replied. "In fact, we did arrest them."

"And they were out on bail before nightfall," Sangremano replied disgustedly. "What's this system of justice coming to?"

"I believe the system of justice has treated you rather well, hasn't it, Mr. Sangremano?" Logan asked. "You've been indicted three times, I believe?"

"And not one conviction," Sangremano said emphatically.

"Yes, sir, that's my point."

"I wasn't convicted 'cause there was no proof that I did what they said I did. These creeps last night admitted they threw the paint. Hell, they bragged about it! They were back out on the streets before my men could even get themselves cleaned up. That's what I mean when I ask what's this system of justice coming to? I'll tell you one thing." Sangremano removed his cigar and waved it around expressively as he talked. "If that bunch of kooks come onto the property again, I'll send them a message they won't soon forget."

"Maybe you've already sent them a message," Cerreta suggested.

"Yeah? What message is that?"

"I don't know. You tell me. Finding a body on your construction site is a pretty powerful message, don't you think? Almost as powerful as the message Chambers Construction Company got when Peter Sondheim was killed," Cerreta said.

Sangremano, who had been leaning forward animatedly, now sat back in his chair. He took a puff of his cigar as he studied the two policemen through squinted eyes. Then suddenly, and inexplicably, he laughed.

"You two guys, you're somethin' else, you know that? You're funnier'n shit. Do you really think I had somethin' to do with killin' that old broad?''

"Did you?"

"Shit. Give me a break, will you?" Sangremano snarled. He took the cigar out and used it as a pointer. "Can I tell you somethin' off the record?"

"Off the record? No," Cerreta said. "That was the whole idea of reading you your rights."

"All right, on the record then, it doesn't matter," Sangremano said, waving his hands. He leaned forward again. "Look, if I had wanted to send a message, I wouldn't have killed some poor, helpless old broad. I woulda killed that sonofabitchin' attorney that got them started in the first place, Hence Fielding. That really would send a message. You know what really gripes my ass? To see Fielding held up as a hero for doing so much for the homeless. Why doesn't someone ask him what he's getting out of all this?"

"What's he getting from all this?" Logan asked.

"Rich . . . that's what he's getting. Plus everybody from the mayor on down is patting him on the back for being such a good and compassionate citizen. You've heard the story of the Pierpont Building, I suppose."

"Yes."

"Of course you have. Everyone has. But now

let me tell you the real story. When the city turned over the deed to the building, the deed didn't go to FACE-IT, it went directly to Hence Fielding. Then Fielding went on TV and to the newspapers, begging for money and material so the poor people could fix up the building for themselves. Hell, even I gave 'em fifty thousand dollars worth of material."

"That was generous of you," Cerreta said.

"Yeah, well, I was able to get a tax benefit from it," he said offhandedly. "And then, I didn't know what a pain in the ass Fielding was going to turn out to be. Anyway, the poor people take all this stuff and fix up the building. Then Fielding arranges all these Title 8 loans so they can buy their own homes, then he sells his interest to a holding company for 2.1 million dollars. Pretty smart, don't you think?"

"Pretty smart," Cerreta agreed.

"Yeah, well, like they say—some steal with a gun, some steal with a fountain pen."

Cerreta stood: "Thank you, Mr. Sangremano, for your time," he said.

"That's all your questions?"

"Yes."

Sangremano smiled and stuck out his hand. "Well, you got anything else to ask, just stop by."

* * *

"He's not our man," Cerreta said as they drove away.

"What makes you so sure?"

"Because he's right. When someone like Sangremano sends a message, it isn't subtle. I believe him. He wouldn't kill one of the indigents —he would kill Fielding, or at the very least, one of the demonstrators."

"So, where do we go from here?"

"I'd still like to find out who the woman was," Cerreta said."

"Mary Mackie," Logan said.

"Except I checked every Mackie in the city and none of them knew anything about her."

"Maybe that guy misunderstood the name. Maybe it's not Mackie. Maybe it's McKay. Why don't we check those names out?"

Cerreta groaned. "Do you have any idea how many McKays there will be? But you're right, it's worth a shot. Okay, let's do it. We'll divide them in half."

Chapter Four

Office of the District Attorney

District Attorney Adam Wentworth had actually started losing his hair when he was very young, and now accepted his state of baldness as a simple fact of life. Nevertheless, he did have a tendency to pat the top of his head frequently, as if keeping his nonexistent hair in place. He was doing this now as he watched a TV news story that he found disturbing. Finally he picked up the phone on his desk and buzzed Ben Stone.

"Yes, Adam?" Stone's voice said.

"Ben, come on into my office, will you?"

"Right away."

As Stone's desk was very near Wentworth's office, it was only a matter of seconds before he was opening the door.

"Watch this with me, will you, Ben?" Wentworth invited.

Stone leaned against the front of his boss's desk and watched the flickering images on the TV screen.

"Authorities are still in the dark as to the identity of the woman whose body was found at the site of the old Bristol Victoria Hotel," the TV reporter was saying. *"The hotel has been completely demolished to make room for new construction. That demolition has been challenged by members of FACE-IT, an organization which assists poor and homeless people to reclaim abandoned buildings. Our Jeanie Bennett spoke with Hence Fielding, founder and head of FACE-IT."*

The opening picture on the screen had been of the demonstrators carrying picket signs in front of the construction site, but after the anchor's introduction, the view switched to a two-shot of a black female reporter and Hence Fielding, the subject of her interview.

"Mr. Fielding, do you believe the woman who was found murdered here, yesterday, had anything to do with the picketing of your people?"

"Absolutely not," Fielding replied. The picture changed to a one-shot, medium close-up of Fielding. His name popped on the screen below him. HENCE FIELDING, HEAD OF FACE-IT. He pushed his glasses back up his nose. *"If it is related to anything,"* he continued, *"it is related to the fact that, once again, society is callously tearing down*

buildings that could be used as shelter for these people."

"These buildings aren't just being torn down for no purpose, Mr. Fielding," Bennett explained. "A new building is going up in its place. I have to tell you that most of the people in this area are very happy with that. It will make an immediate improvement in the neighborhood, create new jobs . . . not just the jobs required for construction, but jobs created by the activities in the building itself. The new construction means shops, offices, and yes, even apartments."

Fielding laughed cynically. "Oh, yes, apartments. I'm sure the homeless here will be thrilled to hear that apartments will soon be available. Do you have any idea what those apartments will rent for?"

"As a matter of fact, I don't," Bennett admitted.

"Neither do I, but I'm certain that some of them will cost more for one month than twenty percent of the people in America earn in an entire year. No, Miss Bennett, don't tell me that Stillman Towers will, in any way, address the needs of these people."

"But on balance, Mr. Fielding, when you consider the opportunities this new building will bring to so many, should progress be halted for the needs of so few? Can we not find some way to accommodate both sides?"

"That's just the point," Fielding said. "There aren't two sides to this issue—there is just one. And that one side is the side of so-called 'progress.' If these homeless people were spotted owls, Miss Bennett, do *you think, for one moment, their habitat would be destroyed?"*

Jeanie Bennett laughed. *"I don't know,"* she admitted.

"Well I do know," Fielding insisted. *"Our nation has reached the point where such things as spotted owls, bald eagles, California condors, and even snail darters—whatever they are—have more rights than people."* He pointed across the street to the construction site. *"If you want to know what killed that poor woman yesterday, I'll tell you. It was societal indifference. Indifference to her suffering and homelessness plagued her during her life. And that same indifference continues now that she is dead. Although the police went through the motions, it's my guess that the investigation is over by now. The authorities are totally indifferent as to what might have happened to her."*

"Do you really believe the police don't care who killed her?" Bennett asked in surprise.

"Do you really believe they do?" Fielding replied. He chuckled cynically. *"I am amazed at your naiveté, Miss Bennett. Not only do they not know, or care, who killed her, they don't even know, or care, who she is. As far as they are concerned, she was just another piece of human offal to be carried off with the daily accumulation of trash. Her passing caused no more note than the fall of a pigeon . . . and considerably less than that of a spotted owl."*

There was a spattering of applause, and the

camera opened wide to show that not only the sign-carrying demonstrators, but also several others, had gathered to watch the interview. By their applause they were showing that they agreed with what Fielding had to say.

The camera returned to a one-shot, this time of Jeanie Bennett.

"The homeless. There are thousands—some say tens of thousands of them in the city. We've all seen them . . . but have we? Don't you, like most of us, look away when you encounter one of them? Do you look into their faces . . . their eyes? Could you describe the last homeless person you saw? Could you identify them, if you saw them again? Chances are you could not, nor could I. We do not see them, because they have become nonentities to us. If a tree falls in a forest and there is no one to hear . . . does that tree make a noise? If a homeless person walks the streets and no one sees them, do they make an imprint? Someone murdered the woman we know only as Mary. Who that someone is, we don't know . . . and we may never know. But the guilt of indifference Mr. Fielding spoke about is the collective guilt of us all. I'm Jeanie Bennett, 'News at Mid Day.'"

Wentworth held up the remote and switched the set off. "I want this one prosecuted, Ben."

"Well, Adam, if they'll make an arrest and give me something to work with, I'll do it," Stone replied. He looked at Wentworth and turned his head slightly, in contemplative study. "What has you so worked up over this one?"

"You heard that report. If the news media decide to become the conscience of society, they'll give us no peace. I would rather move before they force us to." He stroked his chin. "Also, maybe I'm feeling a little guilty. What she said hit pretty close to home. I get so caught up in my own life, and in the affairs of the office, that I do overlook people like that. Let's say an aggressive prosecution might go a long way toward easing my conscience."

"All right, Adam, I'll pay a visit to Cragen to see what they're coming up with," Stone promised.

When Stone went into Cragen's office, Cragen took him back to Cerreta and Logan's desks. There, the two officers, each of whom had open phone books in front of them, were on the phone. Cerreta hung up his phone just as Stone and Cragen arrived. Before he said anything to them, though, he made a slash mark through a name on the page in front of him. More than half the names were already slashed.

"Hello, Ben, what brings you down here with the working people?" Cerreta asked, smiling.

"The D.A. is getting a little antsy about this one," Stone said. "He doesn't want it to slip through the cracks."

"Nobody does," Cerreta said. "But I don't mind telling you, Ben, this one is a ball buster. We don't even know who the victim was, nor do we have the slightest inkling as to why she was killed. That makes finding out who did it all the more impossible."

Logan hung up his phone then, and slashed through another name. "One more down," he said.

"What are you guys doing now?" Stone asked.

Cerreta showed him the telephone pages. "One of the people we talked to said he thought the victim's name was Mary Mackie. We checked all the Mackies, to no avail. Now we're checking the McKays."

"Makes sense," Stone said. "What else do you have?"

"We have a picture of the body, but it's not much to work with," Cerreta said. "However, we did find a picture in her room that we're ninety percent sure is her. Show him the picture, Mike."

Logan opened the file drawer to get the photo.

"So we had the computer people age the photo to what she looks like now," Cerreta continued. "We gave it to our beat cops and they're showing it around, trying to get an ID."

Stone looked at the computer-aged picture. "What did you get this from?" he asked.

Logan showed him the picture they took from the victim's room, of the young woman astride a horse.

"She was pretty," Stone said.

"She was beautiful," Logan said.

"I know where this picture was taken," Stone said.

"You do?" Cerreta asked, his interest heightened by Stone's remark. "Where?"

"At least, I think I do." Stone examined it very closely. "Yes, I'm sure of it," he said. "This is the old Thorngate Riding Academy."

"The Thorngate Riding Academy? I've never heard of that. Where is it?"

"Oh, it's gone now," Stone said. "It went out of business years ago . . . right after I graduated from college, in fact. In its day, though, it was quite well-known. In fact, for the 1964 Olympics, four U.S. riders and one rider from the Canadian equestrian team trained there."

"Say, Phil, why don't we go down to the newspaper morgue and check the sports pages from, say, 1958 to about 1964?" Logan suggested. "Maybe our girl will turn up there."

"We've still got quite a few names to check off here," Cerreta said.

"You two go ahead," Cragen suggested. "I'll

get someone to check out the rest of the names for you.''

''Thanks, Captain,'' Cerreta said. ''Okay, Mike, let's go.'' He laughed. ''But we're going to be looking at the equestrian section and nothing else, okay? Don't start reading sports stories.''

''I'll try and be good,'' Logan promised.

Early Evening, the Newspaper Morgue

Cerreta pulled his eyes away from the micro-film reader and reached around to massage the back of his neck. Logan handed him a cup of coffee and a sandwich, both bought from vending machines.

''How about dinner?'' Logan asked.

''That's what I like about this job,'' Cerreta said as he began to tear open the sandwich. ''We so often get the opportunity to dine in elegant places.'' He pulled back the bread and looked at the filling. ''What is it?'' he asked.

''I don't know,'' Logan said. ''According to the sign on the vending machine, we won't know what it is until the lab report gets back.''

Cerreta chuckled, then took a bite. ''Have you found anything even close?'' he asked.

"No," Logan replied. "To be honest, I've spent the last few minutes reading about the home-run race between Mantle and Maris in 1961. Sure wish I'd been old enough to really enjoy that."

"I was old enough to enjoy it, and it was great," Cerreta said. "But that's not what we're looking for."

"I know, I know. But if you don't want me to get distracted, then have me read something I'm not interested in . . . like the women's page or something."

The idea hit both of them at the same time.

"Damn!" Logan said. "That's it! We're a lot more likely to find her on the women's page."

"All right," Cerreta said, returning to the microfilm reader. "Let's start over."

One Hour Later

"I'll be damned, here she is," Logan said. He pulled away from the reader and offered Cerreta the chance to look.

Though it was a head shot only, the picture was obviously that of the same woman who was sitting on the horse. *Stillman-McCready Nuptials*, the headline above the picture said.

"McCready, not Mackie. Close enough, I can see how the mistake was made. Yes, that's her, all right," Cerreta agreed. "Holy shit, Mike! Did you see who she married?"

"No, I didn't get down that far."

Cerreta pulled away from the reader and looked at Logan with an expression of awe on his face. "She married Arthur Stillman," he said.

"Arthur Stillman? Wait a minute. That's the guy who's building Stillman Towers, isn't it?"

"The same."

"My God, Phil, what have we stumbled into?"

"You're sure of this?" Cragen asked the next morning when Cerreta and Logan went to him with the information. "There's no doubt in your mind that the victim is Mary McCready Stillman?"

"No doubt at all," Cerreta answered. "And if there had been doubt last night, there is none this morning. It turns out that in 1979 Mary Stillman was arrested, booked, and printed for DUI. She didn't spend any time in jail, but her prints are still on file."

"They're a match?"

"They're a match."

Cragen looked at the photo from the newspaper, and the one that had come from the dead woman's room. "This is the same woman, all right," he said.

"Now the question is, what happened to her?" Logan asked. "How did she turn up on skid row?"

Cragen handed the two pictures back. "Maybe that's a question you should ask Mr. Arthur Stillman," he suggested.

"We're going to."

Stillman Executive Offices, Fifth Avenue

Arthur Stillman's office was on the thirty-first floor. Cerreta and Logan shared the "Express to 20" elevator with a few other passengers, but by the time they reached the thirty-first floor, they were the only two left.

When the doors slid open, it didn't let them into a corridor. Instead, they were already in the reception room, with thick carpets on the floor and paneled walls, even a couple of oil paintings, illuminated by recessed lighting.

"Good day, gentleman," a woman said, softly, pleasantly, some forty feet to their left.

"Hello," Cerreta replied. He and Logan started toward the desk.

"How may I help you?" she asked when they got there. She was an attractive woman, confident enough in her appearance that she made no effort to cover the gray streaks in her hair.

"We would like to speak with Arthur Stillman."

The woman frowned slightly. "I don't believe Mr. Stillman is expecting you, is he?"

"No, he isn't," Cerreta said. He showed his badge. "I'm Detective Sergeant Cerreta, this is Detective Logan. We're with the New York Police Department."

"I see," the woman said, reaching for the phone. "May I tell him why you are here?"

"Just tell him it's police business," Logan said.

"Mrs. Arnold, is Mr. Stillman terribly busy at the moment? There are two police officers here who wish to speak with him. Thank you." She hung the phone up and smiled pleasantly. "Mrs. Arnold will be right with you. If you would care to have a seat?" She pointed to a leather sofa and two leather chairs that sat over to one side of the reception area, near a large, smoked-glass window. The seating area afforded a good view of the city's skyline.

They had been sitting for no more than a moment or two when a door at the back of the reception room opened and another woman, an only slightly younger version of the first, stepped through. She smiled pleasantly.

"I'm Mrs. Arnold, Mr. Stillman's executive secretary. Would you two gentlemen like to come with me?" she invited.

Cerreta and Logan followed her down a long, deeply carpeted corridor with more oil paintings on the wall, and then into an office. There was a quiet clack of computer keys being stroked by another woman, whose fingers were flying rapidly over the keyboard and whose eyes were glued to the screen. Mrs. Arnold took them through that office, then pushed open the right-hand side of an ornately carved, Victorian double door, then held her hand out toward the room the doors exposed, inviting the officers in. Inside the room was a large, heavy, teak octagonal table bearing a lamp, three large cut-glass ashtrays, a cigarette box, and a silver table lighter.

"If you'll just have a seat," Mrs. Arnold said, "Mr. Stillman will be right with you. Could I get you something? Coffee? Tea? A soft drink?"

"Thank you, no," Cerreta replied.

After Mrs. Arnold left, Logan growled under his breath, "I think the sonofabitch has something to hide."

"Why?"

"He's going to a hell of a lot of trouble to impress us."

Cerreta chuckled. "Are you impressed?"

"Hell no," Logan replied. Then he too chuckled. "Maybe a little," he said. He sighed. "It must be nice."

"It can't help but make me wonder all the more how, with all this, Mary wound up the way she did," Cerreta said.

"Yeah, I'm wondering about that myself."

A tall, thin man came into the room then. He was wearing heavy-rimmed glasses, their ends lost in the silver hair over his ears. He was wearing a conservative gray suit with a vest, a Phi Beta Kappa key swinging from a gold chain, and a red-and-white diagonally-striped tie.

"I'm Arthur Stillman," the man introduced himself, though as both Cerreta and Logan had seen his picture many times on TV, in newspapers, and even on the cover of national news magazines, no introduction was necessary.

"I'm Detective Cerreta, this is Detective Logan," Cerreta said. "I wonder if we could have a few words with you."

"Yes, I suppose that would be all right."

"It's about your wife, Mr. Stillman," Logan said.

Stillman blinked, and there was a short, almost imperceptible intake of breath.

"There must be some mistake," he said. "My wife is dead."

"Dead?"

"Yes, for nearly twelve years now."

Cerreta and Logan looked at each other for just a moment, as if unsure of themselves, then Logan spoke.

"Mr. Stillman, was your wife's name Mary?"

"Yes."

"Her maiden name was McCready?" Cerreta added.

"Yes, that's right. Mary McCready."

"And you say she's been dead for twelve years?"

"That's right."

Cerreta shook his head. "You'll excuse us for being confused, Mr. Stillman," Cerreta said. "But we're investigating a homicide that happened only two days ago."

"What does that have to do with my wife?"

"That's just it, Mr. Stillman. We've identified the murder victim as Mary McCready Stillman."

"That's impossible. Mary is buried in the Stillman family plot."

"Mr. Stillman, was your wife arrested in 1979 for DUI?" Logan asked.

"I don't— Yes . . . yes, now that I think about it, I believe she was."

"She was fingerprinted then," Logan said. "Those fingerprints are a perfect match with our murder victim."

"But that—that can't be," Stillman said.

"I'm afraid it is. Which brings up the question, who is buried in your family plot?"

Stillman brought a hand to his forehead and squeezed his temples between his thumb and middle finger. He shook his head slowly. "No one," he finally said, very quietly.

"I beg your pardon?"

"No one is buried there," he said again. "There's a marker . . . but no body."

"Why would you do that, Mr. Stillman?"

"Mary left me . . . and our child. I tried everything to find her—lawyers, the police, private detectives. I offered large rewards to anyone who could bring me information about her, but it was as if she had just dropped off the face of the earth. After fifteen years without a trace, I decided she must be dead. I couldn't just leave it in limbo . . . so my daughter and I held her funeral and put up a stone in our family plot. She has been gone for twenty-seven years now. Why, Elizabeth can barely remember her. Where—Where did you find her?"

"She was found by one of the workers at a construction site at Fifty-first and Park," Logan said.

"Fifty-first and Park?"

"Yeah."

"But that's where—" Stillman began, then he stopped and looked at them with his eyes open wide. "My God! That's where Stillman Towers is being built."

"Mr. Stillman, are you saying that you had no idea your wife was still alive? That she was living on the streets?" Cerreta asked.

"At first I suspected that she was living on the streets," Stillman said, "but for some time now I have assumed that she was dead. Putting up the marker over an empty grave was just my way of dealing with it."

"Why did your wife leave a comfortable home to live on the streets?" Logan asked. "I have to tell you, it just doesn't make sense to me."

"No, nor to anyone," Stillman answered. My wife started having . . . problems . . . long before she disappeared for the last time," Stillman began.

"For the last time?" Logan asked.

"Yes. You see, that wasn't the first time she ever disappeared. It happened the first time shortly after our daughter was born. I came home from the office one day to find her gone."

"You mean she abandoned her baby?" Cerreta asked.

"Yes. Well, not completely, we did have a nurse and a maid in the house, so it isn't as if the baby had been left alone. Still, Mary was gone, and I had no idea where."

"What did you do?"

"Well, as you can imagine, I was frantic with worry. I searched everywhere for her . . . called all her friends and family. She wasn't with any of them, and none of them had heard from her. It was nearly a month before she returned."

"Where had she been?" Cerreta asked.

"I never found out," Stillman said.

"Did you try to find out?"

"Yes, of course I did. I begged her, threatened her, I even made her start seeing a doctor."

"What kind of doctor?" Logan asked.

"Dr. Fullman. He's a psychiatrist."

"And did your wife see the psychiatrist?"

"Yes, for well over a year. I thought she was cured, or at least getting better. Then she stopped seeing him and she started disappearing again. At first just for a few days at a time, then for weeks, then finally she left and she never came back."

"And you never heard from her again?"

"No," Stillman said. "As I said, that was twenty-seven years ago. I tried desperately to find her, but I couldn't. Finally, after a period of years, I gave up all hope. I was certain she was dead, and I began thinking of her that way."

"Mr. Stillman, you said you declared your wife dead. Did you have her legally declared dead?" Cerreta asked.

"No," Stillman replied.

"Why not?"

"It just didn't seem the prudent thing to do. I had nothing to prove that she was alive . . . but then, I had nothing to prove that she was dead either. And given her past history, there was still that slim possibility that she was still alive . . . somewhere." Stillman bowed his head and squeezed his temples again. "I even harbored the hope that she might be in the Midwest somewhere, running a small dress shop under another name or something."

"Did you have reason to believe that?" Logan asked.

"Oh, I didn't say I believed that, Detective. I just said I always rather hoped that. It was a much more pleasant alternative than was the life she was actually living."

"Mr. Stillman, you don't have any immediate plans to leave the country or anything, do you?" Cerreta asked.

"No, why?"

"We may have a few more questions later. I'd like to think we could get hold of you."

"I'm not going anywhere, Sergeant," Stillman said. "By the way, where is my wife's body now?"

"She's at the police morgue."

"I would like to have her. I would like to lay her to rest in the place we have kept for her all these years. Do you think that would be possible?"

"I'm sure that can be arranged," Cerreta said. "Thank you for your time."

Chapter Five

Dr. T. J. Fullman looked at his watch as he invited Cerreta and Logan into his office.

"I'm afraid I can only give you a very few minutes, gentlemen. Mrs. Appleby is due at two o'clock, and she is not only very prompt herself, she is extremely impatient with those who aren't."

"We'll try not to take too much of your time, Doctor," Cerreta said. "We would like to talk to you about one of your patients."

"You must know that the patient-doctor relationship is privileged information," Dr. Fullman said.

"We could get a court order, but we're hoping that we won't have to," Cerreta said. "Let us ask you the questions, and if you don't feel it's an ethical violation, you can answer them. If not, then we can take whatever steps are necessary."

"All right, gentlemen, we'll try it that way," Dr. Fullman said. He held up his finger. "But I warn you, the first time I feel I am violating my patient's rights, I will refuse to answer."

"Fair enough," Cerreta said.

"Who is the patient?" Dr. Fullman asked.

"Mary McCready Stillman," Logan said.

"Oh my," Dr. Fullman said. "She was a very special case. A very special case indeed. What is your interest in Mrs. Stillman?"

"She's dead."

Dr. Fullman leaned back in his chair, then he removed his glasses and began cleaning them with a cloth he kept on the desk. "Well," he said hesitantly. "We don't know that, do we?"

"I don't know, she looks pretty dead to me," Logan said.

"You mean, you've seen her? You've actually seen her?"

"Yes," Cerreta replied. "Have you read about the body that was found on the construction site where Stillman Towers is being built?"

"Yes, some unidentified woman," Dr. Fullman replied.

"She isn't unidentified anymore. We have a

positive ID." Cerreta pulled the original and the computer-aged pictures from his pocket and showed them to the doctor. He slipped his glasses back on and looked at them.

"Yes, it's her, all right," he said, handing the pictures back. "What a shame. What a wonderful life she could have had, and how tragically she wasted it."

"That's why we're here, Doctor," Cerreta said. "Why did she waste it? What was it that made a woman with all the opportunities she obviously had, go into the street that way?"

"That's the big mystery," Dr. Fullman answered.

"That's the only answer we get from you?" Logan retorted. "That's the big mystery? I thought you were treating her."

"That was a long time ago."

"Yes, but it started then, did it not, Doctor?"

"Yes. It started then."

"You must have some idea."

"The clinical term is dissociative disorder, or hysterical neuroses, dissociative type."

"Can you put that in simpler terms?" Cerreta asked.

"I'll try," Dr. Fullman said. "A person suffering from this disorder will seem to be distracted, and they'll spend long periods of time just sitting there, totally disassociated with what's going on around them. Perhaps they appear to be watching TV, but they aren't seeing or hearing anything. You can talk to them, and they act as if they don't hear you. When you finally get their attention, it's as if they're having difficulty concentrating long enough to understand what you're saying. At that stage of the disorder, most people tend to shrug it off by saying things like, 'Oh, Mary is always off in her own little world, somewhere.' "

"Yeah, I've got kids like that," Cerreta said.

Dr. Fullman chuckled. "That's a common condition among teenagers," he said. "Nothing to worry about. But when adults do this, and when they slip off into longer and longer stages, then it becomes quite serious."

"Is this anything like Alzheimer's?" Logan asked.

"There are some similarities, I suppose, though Alzheimer's is the result of an insult to the brain, such as multiple ministrokes, whereas dissociative disorder is not. Also, a person with severely advanced Alzheimer's is totally unable to care for himself, whereas in the case of dissociative disorder, the patient can see to their own needs . . . food, clothing when they are cold . . . toilet. But they cannot relate to anyone else, and even close family members might seem like strangers to them. They will go for long periods of time not even certain of who they are, or where they are."

"And Mrs. Stillman was like that?"

"Yes."

"Tell me, Doctor," Cerreta asked. "Shouldn't someone like that be committed to a hospital?"

"Yes, and that was my recommendation," Dr. Fullman said. "But Mary did not want to go, and Mr. Stillman did not have the heart to send her, even though I urged in the strongest possible terms that it would be the best thing for her. In retrospect I should have insisted, even to the point of getting a court order. And, I think when Mr. Stillman saw her the other day for the first time in several years, he finally agreed with me. By then, however, it was too late."

"Wait a minute? Are you saying Stillman saw his wife just a few days ago?" Logan asked.

"Yes, didn't he tell you that?"

"He must have overlooked it," Logan replied dryly.

"Dr. Fullman, besides her husband and daughter, did Mrs. Stillman have any other close relatives?" Cerreta asked.

"There's a brother," Dr. Fullman said. "His name is Byron McCready. You may have heard of him, he's quite a well-known artist."

"Do you know where Mr. McCready lives?"

"Yes, somewhere on Fifth Avenue, I believe. My secretary can give you his exact address."

"Thank you, Doctor, you've been most helpful," Cerreta said.

"Yes, well, I only wish I could have been of more help to poor Mary."

"I thought Arthur Stillman said he hadn't seen his wife in several years," Logan said as he and Cerreta left Dr. Fullman's office.

"That *is* what he said."

"Then he was lying."

"It looks that way."

"You think we ought to have another talk with him?" Logan asked.

"It wouldn't hurt," Cerreta agreed.

Interrogation Room

Cerreta and Logan looked through the one-way glass into the interrogation room. Arthur Stillman was sitting in a chair with his hands folded before him on the table. His lawyer was talking to him, and Arthur was listening intently.

"Are you ready to go in?" Cerreta asked.

"Yeah," Logan replied. "I want to see how the sonofabitch does on our turf, away from all the recessed lighting, paneled walls, and oil paintings."

When they entered the interrogation room, Stillman's lawyer stood.

"Gentleman, I'm Tharon Winchester, Mr. Stillman's attorney," he said. "May I ask the purpose of this meeting?"

"The purpose, counselor, is to ask your client a few questions," Cerreta replied. "Mr. Stillman, you have been made aware of your rights. Would you like to hear them again?"

"That isn't necessary," Stillman replied.

"Sergeant . . . Cerreta, is it?" the lawyer said. "Was it necessary to drag Mr. Stillman down to the police station? Couldn't you have come to his office to ask the questions? He's a very busy man, as I am certain you know."

"Yeah, we know how important he is," Logan said. "We got a look at his office the last time. The only thing is, we didn't get truthful answers to our questions. Mr. Stillman, you told us that you hadn't seen your wife in many years," Cerreta challenged. "Now we find that isn't true. According to Dr. Fullman, you saw her quite recently. We thought we would give you a chance to search your memory for a more truthful answer."

Stillman looked down at the table for a long moment before he replied. "You're right, I wasn't entirely truthful with you. I have seen Mary several times since she left."

"Where? How?"

Stillman shook his head. "I never knew where, how, or when I would see her. She would just show up sometimes. She would wait by my car in the parking garage, she would be standing on the corner, she would come to the back door of the house, late at night. She was always alone, and she always arranged the meetings so that there would be no one else around. And she never wanted Elizabeth to see her."

"Did you ever tell your daughter about the meetings?"

"No. Neither Elizabeth nor Mary's mother, Janet, knew that she was making these periodic visits to see me. For some reason, Mary didn't want them to know, and I honored Mary's feelings on the matter. What was harder for me to do was to not tell Mary anything about our daughter. I tried to tell her when Elizabeth graduated from high school, when she was accepted into law school, but Mary didn't want to hear. She didn't even want to hear about her grandson. To her, it was as if Elizabeth never existed."

"Why would she come to see you?"

"I can't answer that," Stillman said. "Generally, there was never any rhyme or reason to her visits. At first I thought she might be coming to me for money, and I offered it to her, but she rarely ever took more than ten dollars. She told me anyone on the street with more than ten dollars was living dangerously."

"Didn't you ever try to get her to come in off the street?"

"At first I did," Stillman said. "But it was like talking to a fence post. I finally just gave up."

"Mr. Stillman, when did you see your wife last?" Logan asked.

"I'm going to let my attorney answer that question," Stillman said.

"Within the last week, Mr. Stillman saw his wife . . . twice, actually," Winchester said. "He saw her on the nineteenth, and again on the twenty-first."

"You saw her on the twenty-first?" Cerreta said, surprised by the announcement. "You mean you saw her on the night before she was killed?"

"Yes," Stillman replied, answering the question himself.

"Where?"

"In my office."

"Was anyone else there, or was this another one of those secret meetings?"

"I was there," Winchester said.

"Perhaps I should explain," Stillman suggested.

"Perhaps you should."

"When Mary came to see me on the nineteenth, she was upset about the destruction of the Bristol Victoria and the Avery Building, and she wanted me to stop it. In fact, she demanded that I stop it, and threatened legal action if I didn't.''

"What sort of legal action?''

"She believed that she was the actual owner of those buildings, and she claimed that I had no right to do anything there without her permission.''

"Did she, in fact, own the buildings?'' Cerreta asked.

"No. I owned them,'' Stillman said.

"What would make her think that she owned them?''

"Perhaps I can answer your question,'' Winchester said. He cleared his throat. "You see, Mary McCready's maternal grandfather was Jacob Avery. It was he who owned and built both the Bristol Victoria and the Avery Building. He also owned numerous other pieces of property throughout the city. He left the greatest bulk of his estate to Janet, of course, but he left some of his property to Mary's brother, Byron, and he left the Bristol Victoria and the Avery Building to Mary.''

"Then she *did* own the buildings?'' Logan asked.

"Not anymore,'' Winchester answered. "For several years, Mr. Stillman paid the taxes on the property, in Mary's name. Then, after a while, but only when it became evident that Mary was never going to . . . be herself again, he let those taxes go into arrears. When the buildings were put up for sale for the taxes, he paid them, and had the title transferred to his own name."

"Did Mary know that?"

"She did not know it until she came back on Wednesday," Stillman said. "That was when I had Tharon explain it all to her, very carefully."

"Given her condition, do you think she understood it?" Logan asked.

"Detective, don't be misled by Mary's condition," Stillman said. "She suffered from some cruel form of emotional instability, true enough, but she was a very bright person. I wish you had known her before all this happened to her. She was one of the brightest and loveliest women I ever knew."

"How did she react to the news?" Cerreta asked. "Did she get angry?"

"No," Stillman said. "I . . . I would have liked it better if she had. Instead, she just looked at me and said: 'Arthur, you still haven't learned, have you?' For that moment, Sergeant, and for that moment only, she was as lucid as she had ever been in her life. I could see in her eyes that she knew who she was, who I was, where she was, and what had happened to us. It was a haunting moment, and it has been with me ever since."

"What did she mean by, 'You still haven't learned'?"

Stillman shook his head. "I don't know."

"Why did you tell us that you hadn't seen her for several years?" Cerreta asked.

"I don't know. Shame, I guess. I was ashamed that, even though I saw her frequently during all those years, I had never really done anything for her. And I was a little frightened. When you told me you found her murdered on the building site of Stillman Towers, I was afraid that if I told you I had seen her the night before, I would be a suspect."

"Why were you and Mary never divorced?" Logan asked.

Stillman shrugged. "When she first left, I didn't want a divorce. Then, when I realized that the marriage was over, it would have been complicated to divorce her in absentia. Also, my wife was a wealthy woman in her own right, and so much of her holdings were cross-collateralized with mine that it would have been financially inconvenient. Especially as I had power of attorney over her affairs."

"You had her power of attorney?"

"Oh yes, I had complete power of attorney," Stillman said. "She signed it over to me in one of her more lucid moments. And finally, I didn't get a divorce because it was convenient to be married. I, uh, haven't lacked for female companionship, gentlemen. And the relationships I have had were controlled by the fact that I was still, legally, a married man."

"Gentlemen," Winchester said. "I think you can see now that my client has been completely honest and cooperative with you, answering even the most painful of your questions. Surely you don't intend to keep us here any longer."

"I have just a couple more questions," Logan said. He looked directly at Stillman. "Did you kill your wife, Mr. Stillman?"

"No, I did not."

"Do you know who killed her?"

"No, I do not," Stillman said again.

Logan looked over at Cerreta, and Cerreta nodded. "That's all for now," he said.

"Gentlemen, if you intend to have Mr. Stillman return for more questions, please advise me in time to get a criminal lawyer for him. I'm a corporate attorney, you see, and this type of thing is a little out of my field."

"Thank you for your time, Mr. Stillman," Cerreta said.

Logan drummed his fingers on the table as Stillman and Winchester left, then he sighed.

"I'd give my left nut if he was the guy," he finally said. "But I don't think he is."

"No," Cerreta agreed. "I don't either."

"So, what do we do next?"

"Next? We pay a visit to Mr. Byron Mc-Cready."

* * *

There was a small, hand-lettered sign on the door of Byron McCready's apartment. The sign read: PLEASE DO NOT DISTURB ME TODAY. I AM PAINTING. THANK YOU.

Logan, disregarding the sign, rang the doorbell. When the doorbell wasn't answered, he knocked, loudly.

"Mr. McCready? Mr. McCready, open the door, please. We would like to talk to you!" Logan shouted.

After nearly half a minute of loud pounding, they heard a woman's voice call from inside the apartment.

"All right, all right, I'm coming."

The door was opened by a tall, thin, elderly woman. She was wearing a maid's uniform, though Cerreta thought she looked almost too old to be still working in that capacity.

"Didn't you see the sign?" she asked sharply. "Mr. McCready is very serious about interruptions while he is working."

"This is police business," Cerreta said. "Would you please tell Mr. McCready that it's important that we talk to him."

"I'll tell him," the maid said. "He won't be very happy."

"I'm sorry."

"You're sorry. You aren't the one he'll be angry with," the maid said. "Wait here, I'll get him." She turned and walked into the back of the apartment.

A moment later McCready appeared. He was a short, round man with a pudgy face and rimless glasses. He was wearing a painter's smock and holding a paintbrush in his left hand. In his right he cradled a Siamese cat. "Edna told me you were with the police?" he asked.

Cerreta showed his badge. "I'm Detective Cerreta, this is Detective Logan."

"Oh, dear, I do hope Steven hasn't gotten into any trouble?"

"Steven?"

"Steven Jensen, he's my student and protégé. He's a nice young man, but he does tend to get careless at times. I've tried to tell him that I have a reputation to uphold, I can't always be bailing him out of trouble, but you know how young people are. What has he done now?"

"This isn't about Steven," Cerreta said.

"Oh?"

"It's about your sister, Mary."

"Has something happened to Mary?" the maid asked, from across the room.

"Edna, would you please go into another room and let me discuss this with the policemen?" McCready said.

"Yes, Mr. McCready," Edna replied contritely.

"Pay no attention to her," McCready said.

"Mrs. Jackson has been with the family since Mary and I were children." He sighed. "I 'inherited' her, literally. When our mother died, she left explicit instructions in the will that Edna was to have a position in the family for as long as she lived. And since I am the only family left, it has fallen upon me to carry out the terms of the will. Now, what about Mary? Have you found her?"

"Yes."

"Where is she? Do you have her in custody? If so, I'll make all the necessary arrangements to have her transferred to a mental hospital."

"Wouldn't that be her husband's responsibility?" Cerreta asked.

"Normally, I suppose it would," McCready said. "But her husband, and even her daughter, have totally abandoned her. Why, did you know they are so embarrassed by her that they pretend she is dead? They actually had a funeral for her, and there is a tombstone marking her grave in their family plot . . . though of course there's no body in the grave."

"When did you see your sister last?" Logan asked.

"Oh, heavens, I haven't seen Mary in several years," McCready said. "I'd be hard-pressed to tell you just how long. It's been almost thirty years, at least, maybe longer. My sister and I were never very close . . . even before she began to have, uh, problems. And since then, why, the truth is, I doubt that she even remembers that she has a brother."

"Mr. McCready, is this your sister?" Logan asked, showing him the computer-aged photograph.

McCready put down the cat and took the photograph from Logan. He looked at it for a moment. "What is this?" he asked. "It's not an actual photo."

"No, it's been put through a computer process to age it," he said.

McCready handed the picture back. "I believe it is my sister," he said. "I can't be positive. As I said, I haven't seen her in so many years, and I'm sure she has changed considerably from the way she looked then."

"We have made a definite ID. This is Mary McCready Stillman."

"Well, if you say it is, then I won't argue with you. So, what do I do now? Do I need to sign some papers or something to effect the transfer?"

"I'm afraid it's beyond that, Mr. McCready," Cerreta said. "Your sister is dead. She was found murdered a couple of days ago."

McCready sighed. "Oh, poor Mary," he said. He shook his head. "I was always afraid something like this would happen to her. The world is unsafe enough as it is. For a poor woman on the street, it has to be much worse. What are the particulars? Where was she found?"

"She was found on the construction site where Stillman Towers is being built," Cerreta said.

McCready looked up in surprise. "You don't say?" He laughed out loud. "Now, that's a bit of irony for you, isn't it? Does Arthur know?"

"Yes," Cerreta said. "We've spoken with Mr. Stillman."

"I'm sure he's all broken up," McCready said sarcastically.

"Mr. McCready, I know you said you haven't seen your sister in several years. When is the last time you heard from her?"

"Over the years I would get periodic reports that someone had seen her, somewhere. And once, I'm sure I saw her, standing on a street corner."

"Did you try to talk to her?"

"No, why should I? Mary left of her own accord. If she wanted to come back, it was up to her."

"How long ago was that?"

"Oh, heavens, it was before Mother died," McCready said. "And she's been dead now for ten years, or at least it will be ten years on November twenty-sixth."

"But you did know that she was alive all these years?" Logan suggested.

"I thought she might be, though I had no proof of it," McCready replied. "She could have been dead all this time, for all I knew. I did know, however, that she wasn't lying under that tombstone Arthur put up for her. And so you tell me that she is dead. Where is her body?"

"It's in the police morgue, though Mr. Stillman has requested that her body be turned over to him. Have you any objections to that?"

McCready shook his head. "Heavens, no. Arthur has had the place prepared for her for long enough. I guess it's time for her to come home."

"Mr. McCready, aren't you a little curious as to how she was killed? Or who killed her?" Logan asked.

"Do you know who killed her?" McCready asked.

"Not yet," Logan admitted.

"Then it wouldn't do any good for me to be curious, would it?" McCready said easily.

"No, I guess not."

"Gentlemen, will that be all?" McCready said. "I must return to my work."

"That'll be all, for now," Logan said, "though we might want to talk to you again."

"Yes, well, I don't know what for, there is no other information I can give you," McCready replied. "But if you must, you must. Only, please try to keep the disruptions to my painting schedule to a minimum."

"We'll try to remember that," Logan said dryly.

Later, as they waited for the elevator, Logan commented on McCready's reaction to the news. "Talk about the pot calling the kettle black," he said. "McCready made some comment about how broken up Stillman was. What about him? We may as well have told him that it was going to rain tomorrow, for all he cared."

"Yes, well, like he said, he and his sister weren't very close."

The elevator arrived and they stepped on as its only passengers.

"Still," Logan said, continuing the conversation as he punched the button for the lobby. "It seems like McCready could have shown a little something, a little remorse, if not for the woman we found, then at least for the young woman she once was. She was beautiful, classy, intriguing . . . surely he can remember something good about her . . . and miss that."

Cerreta chuckled. "If I didn't know better, Mike, I'd say you were letting this woman get under your skin."

Logan ran his hand through his hair and smiled sheepishly. "I guess I am at that," he said. "It's funny, the influence that picture of her sitting on that horse has had on me. It's like

someone you might see across a crowded room
. . . someone you would like to meet but you
know that, for various reasons, you can't."

Cerreta laughed. "My friend, I never knew
you had such a romantic streak about you," he
said as the elevator doors slid open on the
ground-floor lobby.

Edna, the maid, was waiting there for them.
Seeing her there startled the two detectives
somewhat, for they hadn't seen her leave Mc-
Cready's apartment.

"I heard you tell Mr. McCready that Miss
Mary is dead. Is that true?"

"Yes, I'm afraid it is."

Edna closed her eyes, then crossed herself.

"You knew her?" Cerreta asked.

"Oh yes, ever since she was a little girl. She
was really quite a lovely person when she was
young, but, when her . . . illness started . . .
no one could understand her. No one would
help her. They didn't even try to keep her . . .
not her husband, and not her brother. They
wanted her out of sight, out of mind."

"I suppose a condition like that is very difficult for the family to deal with," Cerreta suggested.

"Yes, I suppose it is," Edna said. "She was
here, you know."

"What do you mean, she was here?"

"She came to speak with Mr. McCready,"

Edna explained. "She was almost like her old self. She knew who she was, she knew who Mr. McCready was . . . why, she even knew who I was," Edna said, beaming. "She said, 'Hello, Edna. How are you?' It was just as if she had only been gone a few days."

"When was she here?" Cerreta asked.

"Why, just three days ago," Edna said. "She came to see Mr. McCready just three days ago." Edna's eyes filled with tears and she raised the hem of her apron to wipe them. "I had hopes that she would be coming back home, where she belongs . . . that she was going to leave that awful street. And now she's dead. Oh, poor Mary. My poor, sweet, Mary."

"Wait a minute," Cerreta said. "You mean she was just here?"

"Yes, sir."

Cerreta and Logan looked at each other. "Would you be willing to testify to that in court?"

"That she was here?" Edna asked. "Of course, why shouldn't I?"

"Because Mr. McCready told us that he hadn't seen her in many years."

"Oh my," Edna said. "Oh my, why would he want to say a thing like that?"

"That's what we'd like to know," Logan said. "Mrs. Jackson, do you know why Mary came to see her brother?"

"Yes," Edna said. She put her hand to her mouth. "Oh, dear, I don't want to get Mr. Mc-Cready in trouble."

"If you have some information that's relative to this case, you must share it with us," Cerreta said.

"Yes, I suppose that is the proper thing to do," the maid said. She sighed. "Mary came to see Mr. McCready, to make him an offer."

"What sort of an offer?"

"Well, I wasn't a party to the conversation, you understand, but I did manage to overhear what they were talking about," Edna said. "Miss Mary offered to withdraw her claim to her mother's inheritance, if Mr. McCready would use his influence to get the construction stopped on the Stillman building."

"Why would she go to her brother?" Logan asked. "Why wouldn't she go directly to her husband?"

"Well, I believe she did go to him," Edna said. "But she told Mr. McCready that he wouldn't listen to her."

"Did McCready offer to help?"

"He said he would speak with Mr. Stillman, but he couldn't make any promises."

"And what was Mary's reaction to that?"

"She said if he wanted her share of the inheritance, he had better make some promises."

"I see. And would that inheritance be worth very much?" Cerreta asked.

"Oh, yes, it would be a great deal of money, I believe," Edna said. "I don't know exactly how much, of course, but I suspect it's more than a million dollars."

"Thank you, Mrs. Jackson," Cerreta said. "You've been most helpful."

Chapter Six

C regan handed the phone over to Cerreta. "It's the D.A. for you, Phil. I asked him to see if he could find out who the lawyer was that represented Janet McCready."

"Thanks, Captain." Cerreta took the phone. "This is Cerreta," he said. "Do you have some information for me?"

"I think so, Sergeant," Wentworth said. "Janet McCready was represented by Barton Fisk of Fisk, Fisk, Elliot and Drumm."

"Okay, thanks, that's a big help," Cerreta said. "Where is their office, by the way? Mike and I will run down there and talk to him."

"Oh, you won't find Barton Fisk at his office anymore, Sergeant. He's retired. Why, I imagine he must be in his mid-to-late nineties by now. I remember having an interview with him when I graduated from college back in the fifties, and it seemed like he was an old man even then.'' Wentworth chuckled. ''But then, everyone seemed old to me at that time in my life.'' He sighed. ''The follies of youth, eh, Sergeant?''

Cerreta chuckled. ''I wouldn't know about that. To tell you the truth, I'm not sure I ever was young. You wouldn't have any idea where Mr. Fisk lives now, would you?''

''I think he has a place out on Long Island somewhere,'' Wentworth said. ''Yes, now that I think about it, I'm sure of it. I got a letter from some fund-raising group out there not too long ago, and they had Barton Fisk's name on the letterhead as one of their officers. I'm not sure of the address, though.''

''We'll find it,'' Cerreta said. ''And thanks for the information.''

''My pleasure,'' Wentworth replied. ''Especially if it will be of any help to you. I really want this case to be made.''

''Believe me, sir, so do we,'' Cerreta replied. He hung up the phone and looked over at Logan. ''Barton Fisk lives out on Long Island. What do you say, Mike? Do you feel like going for a drive?''

''Sure, let's go,'' Logan replied.

Long Island

When they stopped before a small, white frame house, Logan rolled down the window for a closer look. "Are you sure this is it?" he asked.

"Yes, I think so. This is the right address, anyway," Cerreta replied, checking the address on his notebook against the street address of the house.

"It sure doesn't look much like where you would expect to find the retired senior partner of a large law firm, does it?" Logan asked.

"Why not? I think it's a very attractive house."

"It may be, but it isn't exactly what you would call a mansion."

"Maybe Mr. Fisk isn't into mansions."

"Well, let's go have a look," Logan said, getting out of the car. Cerreta got out with him.

Although the house wasn't nearly as large or ostentatious as the houses to either side, it did have a beautifully tended lawn and an exquisite garden. The garden drew their attention first, because there they saw a gardener on his knees, planting bulbs. He was a robust-looking man who Cerreta guessed to be in his late sixties or early seventies. The freshly turned ground behind him attested to the work he had already accomplished this morning.

"Good morning," Cerreta said to the gardener as he let himself through the gate of the waist-high, white picket fence.

"Good morning, gentlemen," the gardener replied, looking up at them and brushing his hands together. "What can I do for you?"

"We would like to speak with Mr. Fisk," Logan said. "Do you know if he's able to receive visitors?"

"Why do you ask such a question? Have you been told he was ill?" the gardener replied.

"No, nothing like that," Logan said. "It's just that he's, well . . . so old. I wouldn't want to impose on him."

"Then why are you here?"

"It's something we would rather take up with Mr. Fisk, if you don't mind," Cerreta said. He showed his badge. "We're with NYPD."

"Is that a fact? Well, we mustn't keep officers of the law waiting, must we? If you would like to come on inside?" the gardener said easily.

"Thank you," Cerreta replied.

Cerreta and Logan followed the gardener into the house. They took a seat in the library and looked around at the pictures and plaques on the wall. The artifacts in the room chronicled what was obviously a long and distinguished career. There were signed photos of Presidents Clinton, Bush, Reagan, Carter, Ford, Nixon, Johnson, Kennedy, Eisenhower, Truman, and Roosevelt. "Look at this one," Logan said, picking up one of the photographs. "This one was of General MacArthur on the battleship *Missouri*, taking the surrender of the Japanese."

"That's me, standing just behind the general," a voice said from behind them. "I had the honor of helping to draft the surrender documents."

Cerreta and Logan turned to look at the man who had just come into the room. To their surprise it was the same man they had spoken to in the garden, though by now he had washed his hands and changed shirts.

"You?" Logan asked. "You're Barton Fisk?"

Fisk chuckled. "I'm sorry if I had a little sport with you out there," he said. "But you were so certain of my infirmity that I couldn't resist it."

"No, sir, I'm the one who should apologize," Logan said. "It's just that I was sure you would be so old that, uh . . ." Logan laughed self-consciously. "I think I'm just making things worse."

Cerreta, who had been taking the entire exchange in with a smile, now chuckled. "Don't mind my partner, Mr. Fisk," he said. "He thinks anyone over fifty is ready for the retirement home."

Fisk laughed good-naturedly. "I suppose ninety-five is quite old, but I'm not going to just lie down because of it. I've given up my legal practice, true enough, but that doesn't mean I have to give up my hobbies. I've gardened for over eighty years, and if I have my way, I'll be gardening on the day I die. Now, gentlemen, what can I do for you?"

"Mr. Fisk, we're investigating the death of Mary McCready Stillman," Cerreta said.

"Oh my," Fisk said. He sighed. "Oh my. Poor Mary. So, she finally succumbed to the rigors of the street, did she?"

"In a matter of speaking, yes, sir. Did you know her?"

"Yes, I knew her. She was a delightful child . . . an excellent rider, by the way. She just missed being selected for the U.S. Olympic team in 1956, did you know that?"

"We found a photograph of her on a horse," Cerreta said. "As a matter of fact, that was how we were able to identify her."

"Where did you find her?"

"She was found on the construction site of a new building, being erected by her husband."

"You have spoken to Arthur, I suppose. And Byron?" Fisk asked.

"Yes, sir. We spoke to both of them. We also believe both of them lied to us."

"In what way?"

"We have evidence that both her husband and her brother saw her recently, though both insisted that they had not seen her in several years."

"Understandable," Fisk said. "On those few occasions when Mary would drop back into their lives from . . . who knows where that troubled woman was, she could be most difficult . . . and embarrassing to her family. She caused her daughter, Elizabeth, a great deal of pain. Arthur tried to spare her as much as he could. . . . He sent her off to boarding schools, then to a fine college. She's a lawyer now, married, and with a child of her own."

"Mr. Fisk, I understand you represented the McCready family," Cerreta said.

Fisk shook his head. "I represented Janet Avery's family," he said. "Then, when Janet married Ian McCready, she asked if I would continue to represent her, and I did so. However, she is the only one of the McCready family that I, or my firm, ever represented."

"But you did make out her will?"

"Yes, I did."

"Offhand, can you remember the provisions of that will?"

"Yes, I can remember the provisions perfectly," Fisk said. He looked at Cerreta and Logan for a long moment. "You know, I suppose I should claim client privilege and all that, but I'm not going to. I'm just too old to play that game. Besides, as I said, my client was Janet Mc-

Cready, and I have a feeling that you suspect that, somehow, her intentions have been thwarted. Therefore, if I cooperate with you, I will be serving her. So, if there is anything I can do to help, I will. Ask away, gentlemen. What do you want to know?''

"Was there a lot of money involved?" Cerreta asked.

"Oh yes, a great deal of money. As I recall, Mary's share at the time the will was probated was eight million dollars. It was placed in escrow for her. With accrued interest, I'm sure the amount has grown considerably.''

"Wait a minute," Cerreta said. "The money was placed in escrow? Why?''

"Those were the terms of the will," Fisk said. "You see, Janet McCready's money was divided into three equal shares. One-third went to Byron McCready, one-third went to Mary's daughter, Elizabeth, and one-third went to Mary. But because Mary's whereabouts was unknown at the time, her third went into escrow, where it was to remain for ten years.''

"What happens to the money after ten years?" Cerreta asked. "Does it go to Elizabeth?''

"No," Fisk said. "It would have gone to the Human Resources Recovery Foundation. That is a charitable organization which assists alcoholics, drug addicts, as well as those who are psychologically disabled, to return to a useful life."

"People like Mary, in other words."

"Yes, the foundation which was to have been the recipient of Janet's charity was not chosen without thought," Fisk said.

"You said it would have gone. What do you mean by that? Won't it go there now that there's proof of Mary's death?" Cerreta asked.

"No, it won't," Fisk said. "According to the will, there was a ten-year period in which Mary could claim her inheritance. If it should be proven that Mary was deceased before that time, then the inheritance would go over to Byron."

"Let me get this straight. If there's proof that Mary is dead before the ten years expires, all the money goes to Byron?" Cerreta asked.

"That's the way the will is drawn," Fisk replied.

"Have the ten years passed?" Cerreta asked.

"No, they have not," Fisk said, stroking his chin and staring off into space. "You can check on it, of course, but to the best of my recollection, Janet died on Thanksgiving day, ten years ago."

"On Thanksgiving day? That's about a month from now," Logan said. "You mean there's only one month left in the ten years?"

"Yes, I think so."

Logan and Cerreta looked at each other for a long moment.

"That means—" Cerreta started, but Fisk completed the sentence for him.

"Since there is now proof of Mary's demise, Byron will inherit the remaining portion of Janet's estate."

Office of the District Attorney

"Byron Lane McCready is heavily in debt," Cerreta said.

"How can that be?" Ben Stone asked. "He inherited a great deal of money, and, as far as we know, he doesn't have an extravagant lifestyle.

"It wasn't wild living, it was poor business," Cerreta replied. "He opened a string of fine-art galleries up and down the eastern seaboard. He has one in Boston, one here, one in Philadelphia, another in Baltimore, and one in Charleston, South Carolina. For a while there, while the Japanese were inflating art prices, the galleries were going great guns . . . then the art market went soft and the McCready Galleries were stuck with a lot of overpriced art. If he doesn't come up with six million dollars by the end of the year, he will lose everything."

"He has to come up with six million?" Stone asked. He gave a low whistle. "How would you like to have that hanging over you?"

"Yeah, that's what I was thinking," Cerreta replied. "Something like that might make a man look for another source of funding."

"The escrow account," Stone said.

Cerreta nodded affirmatively. "Which, at the moment, has more than thirteen million dollars on deposit. That amount of money would have to be awfully tempting."

"All right, I'll grant that he had motive," Stone said. "But we can't indict on motive."

"What about the fact that he lied?" Logan asked. "He told us that he had not seen, spoken to, or heard from his sister in several years. Yet the maid swears that she came to see him just a few days before she was killed."

"Arthur Stillman also swore that he hadn't heard from her for several years," Paul Robinette put in. Robinette was Stone's partner. He was young, very bright, black, and ambitious. "But it turned out he had been seeing her all along."

"Arthur Stillman didn't have a reason to want Mary dead. Byron McCready did," Logan replied.

"Exactly my point," Robinette explained. "Stillman had no reason to want Mary dead, and yet he lied about having seen her. What would make a jury believe that McCready's reason for lying was any more sinister than Stillman's?''

Cerreta smiled. "There is a difference," he said. "Besides possible motive."

"What?" Stone asked.

"We found McCready's fingerprints in Mary's room," Cerreta said. "We didn't find Stillman's."

"How did you match McCready's fingerprints?"

"When we showed McCready the computer-aged photograph, he left his fingerprints on it. We got a perfect match between those prints and some of the prints we found in Mary's room. Not only did Byron McCready hear from his sister—he was in her room at the old Avery Building."

"Now we have motive and opportunity," Logan said.

Stone stroked his chin for a long time, considering the information.

"Can you get witnesses?" Robinette asked.

"Come on, to the murder?" Logan replied. "Be reasonable, Paul, you're asking for the impossible. Why not just wait until we have a signed confession?"

Robinette shook his head. "No, not to the murder. Just someone who can place McCready there."

"Hell, I thought the fingerprints did that," Cerreta said.

"The fingerprints will put him there, all right," Stone said. "But they don't tell us *when* he was there. Paul is right. If you can find a witness who will place Byron McCready at the scene of the crime at approximately the right time, we'll go to the grand jury."

"All right," Cerreta said. "You want witnesses, we'll get witnesses. Come on, Mike, let's get started."

"Credible witnesses," Stone reminded them.

"Credible witnesses," Cerreta called back over his shoulder.

"Great," Logan said. "Now all we have to do is the impossible."

"Maybe not so impossible," Cerreta suggested.

Logan looked over at his partner. "What? You have an idea?"

"You remember when we interviewed Sister Theresa? She said she saw someone with Mary that night, after supper. Someone who was arguing with her."

"Yeah? You think it was Byron?"

"There's one way to find out. We'll bring Byron McCready in to stand in a lineup."

"Yeah," Logan said. "It's worth a shot."

The Lineup

There were six men standing in front of the lineup wall. Three were policemen, one was a janitor who was often used for such duty, one was a filing clerk, and one was Byron McCready. Byron had an expression of anxious anger on his face, but that expression was matched by the others, who had done this often enough to be able to portray anything from fear to nonchalance, according to the needs of the occasion.

Cerreta and Logan took Sister Theresa into a dark room adjacent to the lineup room. The lineup room was brightly lighted, and the participants could be clearly seen through a large, glass window, which covered most of one wall.

"If you would just stand here, Sister," Cerreta said. "You will be able to see them quite clearly, but they can't see you."

"Yes, I understand," Sister Theresa said. "I've seen this done on TV."

Logan picked up a microphone, which transmitted his voice into the brightly lighted room. "You people in the lineup, stand straight, please, and look to the front."

"I . . . I think I see him," Sister Theresa said.

"Now, be very certain," Cerreta cautioned.

"Turn to the right, please," Logan said into the microphone, and everyone on the lineup complied.

"Take your time," Cerreta said.

"Turn all the way around and face to the left, please," Logan said.

"That's him, I'm certain of it," Sister Theresa said. "This was exactly the angle he was standing when he was arguing with Mary."

"Which one is it, Sister?"

"Number five," Sister Theresa said confidently.

Cerreta and Logan smiled at each other. Number five was Byron McCready.

"All right," Cerreta said. "If Sister saw him, then so did someone else. Let's get back down there and find a few more."

Executive Assistant District Attorney's Office

"Ben, do you have a minute for Logan and me?" Cerreta asked, sticking his head in through the assistant D.A.'s door.

"Sure," Stone answered. "What's up?"

"We have four witnesses who can place Byron McCready on the scene the night his sister was killed."

"Are they credible?"

"We brought one of them with us so you could judge for yourself," Cerreta said. He looked back at Logan and nodded, and a second later Logan came in, leading a young woman. Seeing her, Stone stood up.

"This is one of them," Cerreta said, smiling broadly. "Her name is Theresa. *Sister* Theresa," he added. "Is that credible enough for you?"

Ben chuckled. "You won't get any argument from me," he said. He turned to the nun. "Sister Theresa, you saw Byron McCready in the Avery Building?"

"No," Sister Theresa answered.

Ben looked at Cerreta and Logan with an expression of confusion. "What is this?" he asked. "I thought she could put him in the building."

"She can do better than that," Logan said, smiling broadly. "Tell him, Sister."

"I did not see Mr. McCready in the building," Sister Theresa said. "But I did see him with Mary."

"What? You saw him with Mary? When?"

"On the night before she was killed," Cerreta said. "A little after seven."

"Any possibility of a foul-up on the ID?" Stone asked.

"I don't see how. She picked him out of a lineup," Cerreta said. "It was a clean look, no pictures or descriptions beforehand."

"What about it, Ben? Is it enough? Can we indict?" Logan asked.

"As far as I'm concerned we can, but let's take it to Adam," Stone said. He smiled again at Sister Theresa. "Thank you, Sister, you have been very helpful."

"I'll walk you back to the elevator," Logan offered.

As Sister Theresa left, Stone picked up the phone and punched Wentworth's number. "Adam, we might be ready to move on the Mc-Cready case." He paused for Wentworth's response, then he continued, "Okay, fine, we'll be right in." Hanging up after speaking with Wentworth, he called Robinette. "Paul, we've got a witness in the McCready case." He smiled at something Robinette said. "What? Oh, yes, I think she'll be believable. Cerreta and Logan and I are going to see Adam about it now. Why don't you come with us?"

Adam Wentworth sat on the leather sofa in his office and studied the folder Stone had given him. Stone leaned against the bookcases on one wall, with his arms folded across his chest, watching. Robinette and Cerreta were sitting in leather chairs on the other side of the coffee table. Logan was leaning against the front of Wentworth's desk. After studying the file for a few moments, Wentworth looked up.

"We still haven't found the murder weapon?" he asked.

"No," Cerreta admitted. "From the wound residue, we believe it was a heavy piece of iron . . . possibly a pipe, or something like that. But so far we've been unable to locate it."

"Also, as you can see, she was killed by a crushing blow to the right side of her head," Logan pointed out.

"Which means the murderer was probably left-handed," Robinette added.

"And Byron McCready is left-handed," Stone concluded.

"So are a lot of people," Wentworth said.

"Yes, but a lot of people weren't seen with the victim a few hours before her death," Logan said. "McCready was."

"And how about this?" Stone put in. "In addition to the ferrous oxide, Forensics also found traces of turpentine in the wound."

"Turpentine? Is there supposed to be something significant in that?" Wentworth asked.

"We think so," Logan answered. "Byron McCready is a painter. Painters use turpentine."

"Adam, we have motive," Stone said, holding out his hand to enumerate the points on his fingers. "According to Janet McCready's will, if there is proof of Mary McCready's death before November twenty-sixth, Byron McCready inherits everything. If there is no proof of Mary Mc-

Cready's death, or if she did not claim her inheritance before November twenty-sixth, it would all go to charity." He held up his second finger. "We have opportunity. Byron Mc-Cready's fingerprints have been found in Mary's room, and one of the nuns, as well as a few others, can put Byron with Mary just before she was killed." He held up a third finger. "And, we have physical evidence which points to Byron McCready . . . the fact that her killer was left-handed, and the traces of turpentine which were found in the victim's wound."

"None of which is conclusive," Wentworth said.

"We've gone to trial with less," Stone reminded him.

"I don't know," Wentworth said. "You know, when this all started, I thought we were dealing with one of our city's unfortunate. I wanted the case made because I wanted to prove to certain vocal elements that violent crime will not be tolerated no matter who it is against. Now, however, it turns out that we are dealing with some of the wealthiest and most powerful people in the city. You know what's going to happen, don't you, Ben? This is going to turn into one of those circuses where the case is tried and retried on the national news every night. There will be legal 'experts' criticizing our every move."

"We won't be trying it before the pundits,

Adam," Stone said. "We'll be trying it before a jury in a court of law."

Wentworth looked up at Stone. "Thank you for that bit of reassurance, counselor," he said sarcastically.

"I'm sorry, Adam, I didn't mean that the way it sounded," Stone apologized. "It's just that I think we have a good case here, and I would feel comfortable presenting it to anyone."

Wentworth sighed and closed the folder. "All right," he said, handing the folder back to Stone. "Go for Murder Two. But call him in and talk to him first. If you can get him to plead Man One, take it. I have a feeling this is going to be a harder case to make than you realize."

Chapter
Seven

Interrogation Room

Allison McKenzie used her exceptional
beauty as just another tool of her trade.
When she felt that someone might not
take her seriously if she were too pretty, she
would play it down. On the other hand, if she
felt her looks could work to her advantage, she
was more than willing to accent her many
charms.

It was obvious from her appearance this afternoon, however, that she thought her position
would be improved by appearing more business-
like. To that end, she had her naturally blond
hair pulled back into a severe bun, she was wearing oversized glasses and a minimum amount of
makeup. Despite her efforts, however, she could

still turn men's heads anytime she walked into a room, be it a conference room or an after-hours bar.

As far as Stone was concerned, it didn't really matter how Allison looked. He didn't have any misconception about her intelligence or her legal skills. He had seen her work before, and he had seen her chew up adversaries who didn't take her seriously enough. In fact, if the situation were ever to occur where he needed a good defense attorney, she would be very high on his list of candidates.

"You have to be grasping at straws, Ben," Allison said. "You don't have anything, and you know it. I don't know why you even bothered to call us in for this little talk."

"We have enough to get an indictment for Murder Two," Stone said.

"Getting an indictment isn't getting a conviction," Allison said. "The D.A. owns the grand jury. You know it and I know it. But when you try to plead this before a courtroom jury, you're going to find that it's a whole new ball game."

"If you want us to take our case before a jury, counselor, we'll be pleased to do so," Stone said. "We have McCready's fingerprints in his sister's room, we have eyewitnesses who saw them together on the night of the murder, we have the M.E.'s report which indicates that the victim's assailant, like Byron McCready, was probably left-handed. And we have Janet Mc-Cready's will, which states that Byron McCready stands to inherit a great deal of money now that his sister is dead before the expiration date in November. We believe Byron McCready killed his sister. And I would also ask you, counselor, to bear in mind that we aren't dealing with degrees of shading here . . . no self-defense, no fits of passion, no extenuating circumstances of any kind. It was murder for profit, pure and simple, and it has been my experience that juries don't look too kindly upon people who murder for profit. Now, are you sure you want to subject your client to that? Or, wouldn't you rather deal?''

"Hold on here, what is this?'' Allison asked. "What are you telling me, Ben? Are you saying that, despite all this massive evidence and your enormous confidence, you would still be willing to deal?''

"We are prepared to offer Man One if your client will save us the time and expense of the trial.''

Allison laughed; a low, throaty laugh. "Oh, I'm sure you would. But I certainly wouldn't want to miss the opportunity of seeing this case in court, now, would you? I think it's going to be a fascinating trial,'' she added. "Not only that, I imagine a lot of people are going to be interested in this case. I don't think we should let them down."

"Surely, Allison, you aren't going to let the prospect of a little publicity cloud your judgment," Ben said. "Take the deal while it's still on the table."

"Thank you for your concern, Benjamin, but you have just made my point," Allison replied. "If you really did have us as dead to rights as you claim, you wouldn't even be talking to us about a deal. You'd be loading up for the big kill."

"We're already loaded," Stone said.

"Are you? Well, take your best shot, Ben, but don't be surprised if you wind up shooting blanks."

Superior Court, November 9

Stone watched Allison McKenzie walk across the courtroom to take her place at the defense table, her easy gait as sensual but unselfconscious as a lithe teenager's. She took her chair and crossed her long legs in one easy, unbroken movement. Chameleonlike, she had made another adjustment in her appearance. Her hair wasn't pulled back in a bun today. Instead it was a lion's mane of spun gold. And the oversized horn-rimmed glasses she had been wearing in the interrogation room were gone as well, replaced by contact lenses. It was almost as if Allison McKenzie had two distinct personalities, and Stone couldn't help but wonder if the "mousy-librarian McKenzie" would make another appearance if it proved necessary.

"All rise!" the bailiff called. "Oyez, oyez, oyez, the Superior Court in and for the State of New York is now in session, the honorable David Crader, presiding.

"She doesn't miss a trick, does she?" Stone asked under his breath.

"What's that?" Robinette asked.

"If there's a bigger womanizer on the bench than David Crader, I'd like to know who it is," Stone said. He looked over at Allison and smiled, letting her know that he knew she was playing to the judge's lecherous tendencies. She smiled back, letting him know that she knew he knew, and that there was nothing he could do about it.

"She's not very subtle about it, is she?" Robinette asked.

"Don't complain too much, Paul. If Allison McKenzie thought it would give her an advantage, she would come to trial in pasties and a G-string."

Robinette chuckled. "You know, it would almost be worth it."

"Et tu, Brute?" Stone teased.

The first order of business was the selection of jurors. Even in this, the defense counselor exercised a subtle, but very real effect on the jury selection, because Stone found himself facing one additional consideration. Would a male juror likely be more sympathetic to a case argued by a beautiful woman? Would a female juror likely be less sympathetic for the same reason? On the part of the female jurors, however, he also had to consider the aspect of gender pride. For example, would the fact that defense counsel was a woman play enough of a role to offset what might otherwise be a put-off from the defense counsel's extraordinary beauty? All this was in addition to the normal considerations one had in selecting a jury.

"Look at her work," Stone said under his breath as Allison questioned a prospective juror, an overweight, gray-bearded man who was obviously taken by her charms. He was, however, one of the jurors Stone thought he would like to keep.

"I don't have to look," Robinette answered. "The judge is looking enough for both of us."

When Stone saw how intently Judge Crader was watching Allison, he groaned. "My God, he's practically undressing her. All we need now is a burlesque band with blaring horns, clashing cymbals, and banging rim shots.''

Though Stone didn't speak loudly enough for anyone but Robinette to hear, Judge Crader suddenly cast a long, disparaging look at him, as if he had heard. Smiling, Stone nodded at the judge, and the judge finally looked away.

It took a day and a half to select the jury, but just after lunch seven women and five men were sworn in and seated. Judge Crader looked over at Allison McKenzie.

"Is the prosecution ready?"

"The State is ready, Your Honor," Robinette answered.

"Defense?"

"The defendant is ready, Your Honor," Allison replied.

Crader leaned back in his chair and folded his arms across this chest. "Then let us begin, shall we? The State may present its opening statement."

Stone stood up and walked toward the jury. "If the court please," he said. "Ladies and gentlemen of the jury, a little over two months ago, a worker on a construction site found a woman's body. She was a member of this city's shadow society. She was a street person, one of those people who occupy the same time and place as do the rest of us, while at the same time existing in a universe so foreign to our own that we can pass them on the street without even seeing them.

"At first the worker thought perhaps she had died of exposure, malnutrition, disease, or one of the many other dangers that afflict such people. Then he saw that her death wasn't natural at all. She had been murdered, brutally clubbed to death with blows so powerful that half of her head was literally crushed.

"Who would murder such a person? What would they have to gain by such an act?

"Let me answer that by saying that the murder of indigents is not rare. They are killed for any number of reasons. . . . In the case of women, they are sometimes raped and murdered. Sometimes they'll be killed by another indigent for something as ordinary as a pair of shoes, gloves, a scarf, or a blanket. It pains me to say that they are even killed by thrill-seekers who ascribe no more humanity to a street person than they would to an insect.

"The State of New York does not think of a street person as something less than human. I certainly don't think of a street person as something less than human, and I'm sure you don't either. When such a person is murdered, our legal system has as much obligation, authority, and eagerness, to see that justice is done as we would have if the victim happened to be a member of one of the most socially prominent families in the city."

Here, Stone paused, then he turned and looked for a long, pregnant moment across the courtroom toward the defendant's table. He stared pointedly at Byron McCready. Then he turned back to the jury.

"Ladies and gentlemen of the jury, the case we are trying today is particularly unique because it covers both ends of the scenario I have just presented. Mary McCready Stillman, the victim, was a member of that shadow society. For nearly twenty years she was on the street, living through cold nights and hungry days, facing hardships that we can't even imagine. She was, in every sense of the word, a member of the shadow society. And yet . . ." Stone held up his index finger, then he turned again toward the defendant. "And yet, ladies and gentlemen, she was, by birth and by marriage, a member of this city's most advantaged society. Like the defendant—her brother, Byron McCready—Mary inherited a great deal of money from her mother.

"For reasons that we do not understand, Mary turned her back on that life and on that money. While she stood in soup lines at charity kitchens, millions of dollars languished, unclaimed, in an escrow account, drawing interest, compounding, and growing day by day, month by month, and year by year.

"Byron McCready inherited an equal amount of money from his mother, but Mr. McCready, through unwise business investments, squandered it all. As a result of this, we have the sister who has money but does not want it, while at the same time there is a brother who wants money but does not have it.

"Now, what about this money in the escrow account? Before I can explain it to you, you must first understand why the money was left in escrow. You see, at the time of Janet McCready's death, she had not seen nor heard from her daughter for many years. Janet wasn't even sure as to whether her daughter was dead or alive. That left her with a dilemma. If her daughter was alive, she did not want to exclude her from her rightful inheritance. If, on the other hand, her daughter was dead, then she wanted the money to go to her son Byron. So she added a codicil which, prosecution believes, was ultimately the reason for Mary McCready Stillman's death."

Stone returned to the prosecutor's table and picked up a document, slipped on his glasses and began to read:

" 'That portion of my estate which is reserved for my daughter Mary shall await her claim for a period of ten years. If the ten years shall pass without a claim made by my daughter, then it is my desire that the money be donated to the Human Resources Recovery Foundation to be used to assist alcoholics, drug addicts, and others who are psychologically disabled. I do this with the hope and prayer that such an investment will, in some way, directly or indirectly, benefit Mary.

" 'However, if there shall be proof of my daughter's demise prior to the expiration of the ten-year period herein mentioned, all money and property designated as my daughter's share shall be given over to my son, Byron.' "

Stone lay the paper down and removed his glasses, then looked back at the jury. "Mary Mc-Cready Stillman's body was found on September twenty-second of this year. The ten-year period specified in Janet McCready's will expired on November twenty-sixth of this year, meaning that there was only one more month remaining before the money would have gotten away from Byron forever. It is not hard, ladies and gentlemen of the jury, to understand Byron Mc-Cready's motive for wanting his sister dead. We will also introduce evidence and eyewitnesses to show that Byron McCready was with his sister on the night she was murdered. Defense is going to remind you that you must be convinced, beyond a shadow of a doubt, as to the guilt of Mr. Mc-Cready before you can find him guilty. I stand here before you now to tell you that you don't need that reminder. I will tell you that myself, for I am absolutely convinced that we will be able to make our case. By the end of the trial there will be no doubt in your minds. You will be able, with a clear conscience, to return a verdict of guilty.''

When Stone returned to his seat, Judge Crader looked over at the defense counsel. ''Miss McKenzie, does Defense have an opening statement?''

''A very brief one, Your Honor,'' Allison replied. She stood up and looked toward the jury, but she did not leave her place at the table. ''I'll not be making a traditional opening appeal,'' she said. She smiled at Stone. ''For one thing, my learned colleague has already reminded you of the most important tenant of the American judicial system. As of this moment, Mr. McCready is innocent of this charge . . . and he will remain innocent, until it is proven, beyond the shadow of a doubt, that he is guilty. Prosecution has that burden of proof. We intend to let them try to make their case, while we shall be challenging and refuting every point they make until they have nothing left. Then, when their case lies exhausted and discredited upon the ground, you will be able to, using my colleague's own words, 'in clear conscience' render a verdict. And the verdict you will return will be 'not guilty.' ''

Allison sat back down.

"Prosecution may call your first witness," Judge Crader said.

Robinette stood up. "Your Honor, the State calls Jim Siffer to the stand."

Jim Siffer, dressed in a blue suit and with a fresh haircut, took the oath, then sat down. Robinette opened the examination.

"Mr. Siffer, what is your occupation?"

"I am an equipment management specialist for the Sangremano Construction Company."

"That is the company that is working on the Stillman Towers project?" Robinette asked.

"Yes."

"On the morning of September twenty-second, Mr. Siffer, did you have occasion to arrive on the work site before anyone else?"

"Yes, sir, I arrive first every morning. My job is to see what equipment is being used, how much longer it will be needed, and how soon they will need something else."

"What time did you arrive on the site?"

"Between six-thirty and seven."

"Take us step by step through the next few minutes, will you?" Robinette asked.

"Well, sir, I parked my truck on the sidewalk. Uh, I have a permit for that, it helps to keep down the congestion in the street. Part of our crane reaches out into the street, and we have an air compressor and generator that sits there all the time. Then, too, there are the demonstrators. They're there before I arrive even, and one of them was already there that morning, standing in the middle of the street, handing out those damn circulars. I'm sorry, I guess I'm gettin' a little off track, but it helps me to think if I put it all together like that."

"That's all right," Robinette said. "Go on with your story. I want you to be as accurate as possible."

"Well, sir, after I parked the truck, I stepped through the fence and onto the site. I started checking the usage logs of the equipment to see if any of them had developed any problems durin' the day before. Then, when I walked over to look at the five KW generator, that's when I saw it."

"What did you see?"

"I saw legs sticking out from the angle formed by sheet metal leaning against a wall. To be honest, I thought it was just one of the street people sleeping it off. I tried to wake them up, then I discovered that the person was dead."

"What did you do next?"

"I didn't touch the body or anything. I went back out to the truck to use the cellular phone. I called the police first, then I called my office to tell them about it. After that I just waited for the police to show up."

"Mr. Siffer, I show you this picture, and ask you if it is the body you discovered."

Siffer looked at the eight-by-ten exhibit, then nodded his head.

"Yes, sir," he said. "That's her."

"Let it be shown that the body Jim Siffer found and has identified is that of Mary McCready Stillman," Robinette said. "Thank you, Mr. Siffer. No further questions."

"Cross-examination, Miss McKenzie?" Judge Crader asked.

Allison walked over to stand between the witness and the jury. "Mr. Siffer, when you called in your report, you didn't say you had found a woman's body, did you?"

"No, ma'am," Siffer replied.

"What did you say?"

"I said I'd found a man's body," Siffer said. "I didn't realize it was a woman until after the police came."

"Why not?"

"She was wearing men's clothing," Siffer said. "Also she wasn't very . . . well, the truth is, you had to look really close to tell."

"No further questions, thank you, Mr. Siffer."

"Redirect?" the judge asked.

Paul Robinette stood, but he didn't leave the table. "Mr. Siffer, there is no doubt in your mind, is there, that the body you discovered and the body in the photograph are one and the same?"

"No, sir, there is no doubt at all," Siffer said.

Siffer's testimony was followed by testimony from the first police officers who arrived on the scene, and by both Cerreta and Logan, the detectives who worked the case. They were followed by Dr. Henry Baker, the pathologist who examined the body. Dr. Baker's testimony, sparing none of the gory details, concluded with the observation that the assailant was probably left-handed.

"Why do you suggest that the assailant may have been left-handed?"

"Because the wound is to the right side of the victim's head," Dr. Baker explained.

"Did you find any foreign residue in the wound, Doctor?" Stone asked.

"I did."

"What did you find?"

"The two most obvious things were flakes of iron rust and some sort of cloth fiber."

"Was there anything significant about the iron rust flakes?"

"They were embedded deep into the wound," Dr. Baker said. "Consistent with the residue which would be left from an iron instrument being used as a club."

"Other than the obvious rust flakes and the cloth residue, were there any other foreign substances in the wound?"

"Nothing visible to the naked eye," Dr. Baker

replied. "But I did take scrapings, and I transmitted those scrapings to the forensic lab."

"Thank you, Doctor, I have no further questions," Stone said.

"Miss McKenzie," Judge Crader invited.

"Thank you," Allison said. She walked over to the witness stand. "Now, Dr. Baker, you stated that you believe the victim was murdered by a heavy iron object, is that correct?" Allison asked.

"Yes."

"Have the police brought the weapon to you for identification?"

"No."

"In fact, Dr. Baker, to your knowledge, have the police even found the weapon?"

"No."

"You also stated your belief that the killer was a southpaw?"

"I beg your pardon?"

"Excuse the baseball terminology, Doctor," Allison said. "I mean left-handed. You stated your belief that the killer was left-handed."

"Yes."

"How did you come to this conclusion?"

"Well, because the blows came to the right side of the victim's face and head. That would mean the killer would be swinging . . ." He held up his hand, then hesitated.

"That's all right, Doctor, go ahead, demonstrate," Allison said.

With his hands together as if holding a weapon, Dr. Baker brought his hands across, left to right.

"Dr. Baker, it wasn't just a slip of the tongue a moment ago, when I used a baseball term," Allison said. "I am, in fact, a great baseball fan. I particularly follow the New York Yankees, and I would like to ask if you have ever heard of a one-time Yankee baseball player named Roger Maris."

"Yes, of course. Sixty-one home runs in 1961," Dr. Baker said. "As a matter of fact," he added, "I saw him hit ten of them."

"Did you? That must have been exciting. I would like to have seen him play," Allison said. "I've seen films of him, of course. Interesting, don't you think, that he threw with his right hand, he wrote with his right hand, in fact, he did everything with his right hand except hit? Roger Maris hit from the left side of the plate. Were you aware of that, Dr. Baker?"

"Uh, yes, now that you mention it, I believe he did."

"Well, if a right-handed person like Roger Maris could hit with his left—well enough to hit sixty-one home runs—then don't you think it would be possible for the person who killed Mrs. Stillman to also be right-handed?"

"Well, uh, yes, I suppose the killer could be right-handed," Dr. Baker said.

"Then again, you may have been correct in your original observation . . . the killer might have been left-handed," Allison said. "Oh, by the way, Doctor, did you find anything that would prove, conclusively, that the killer was male?"

"No."

"Did you find anything that would prove, conclusively, that the killer was Caucasian?"

"No."

"Did you find anything that would prove, conclusively, that the killer was of any particular racial or ethnic group?"

"No."

"Did you find anything that would establish, conclusively, the killer's age?"

"Again, my answer would have to be no."

"Then, let's sum it up, shall we, Dr. Baker?" Allison said. "What you are saying is, the killer could be man or woman, black or white, Hispanic or Asian, old or young, left-handed or right-handed. Is that pretty consistent with your findings?"

"Uh, yes, I guess so," Dr. Baker stammered.

"Dr. Baker, that narrows it down to just about four billion people, doesn't it?"

The gallery laughed.

"I, uh, suppose it does," Dr. Baker mumbled.

"Thank you, Doctor, I have no further questions."

"Dr. Baker," Stone said. "We could spend the rest of the day asking questions about what we don't know. Let's get back to the basics, the things that we do know. We know without a doubt that the victim is dead. Is that correct?"

"Yes, sir, I would say so."

"Was there anything to suggest that the victim might have died of natural causes?"

"No. Cause of death was the head trauma."

"In your expert opinion, Doctor, could that head trauma have been caused by accident?"

Dr. Baker shook his head. "Absolutely not. The wounds are totally inconsistent with accidental death."

"How many murder victims have you examined over the course of your career, Dr. Baker?"

"Oh, heavens, I don't know . . . I couldn't even begin to estimate."

"Would it be fair to say that you have examined more than one hundred?"

"Many times that."

"And how many of them have displayed wounds similar to the wounds presented by this case."

"Well over one hundred."

"So, based on your experience and expertise,

you are prepared to say, without hesitation, that Mrs. Stillman was a victim of murder?''

"There is no doubt in my mind," Dr. Baker said.

"And you also believe that she was killed with a bludgeon of some sort?''

Dr. Baker nodded. "Yes, made of iron," he said. "Possibly an iron pipe or bar."

"We have a murder victim and we have a partial description of the murder weapon. All we need is the murderer," Stone said. "Now, I'm not asking you to consider every left-handed, right-handed, male or female, old or young, black, white, Hispanic or Asian person in the entire world, Doctor. I am only asking you to consider one man: Byron McCready. Is there anything in your findings that, in your mind, would eliminate Byron McCready as a suspect?''

"No."

"Thank you, Doctor. No further questions."

"You may step down, Dr. Baker," Judge Crader said.

After Dr. Baker, there was testimony from the police officer who was in custody of the evidence from the time it left the morgue until it was delivered to the forensic lab. His unchallenged testimony established that, under the rules of evidence, there was no broken chain in the custody of the evidence examined by the forensic lab.

After the police officer's testimony, Stone called Dr. Daniel Fenton to the stand.

"Dr. Fenton, you are a doctor in physical science, forensics?"

"Yes."

"Would you please tell the court the schools you attended, what degrees you have attained."

"My undergraduate work was at Southeast Missouri State University, with a degree in criminology. I did my masters program at Northwestern University, and my doctorate in physical science, forensics, at Columbia University."

"Dr. Fenton, you are now with the forensic lab of the New York Police Department, are you not?"

"Yes, I am."

"In what capacity?"

"I am the senior lab technician."

"How long have you occupied this position?"

"How long have I been the senior technician, or how long have I been in the forensic lab?"

"Both."

"I have been in the lab for twenty-three years. I have occupied the senior position for seven years."

"In addition to your position with the New York Police Department, you are also a professor of forensic science at NYU?"

"Yes, I am. I have been teaching at NYU for fourteen years."

"And you are published in the field of forensics?"

"Yes, I've had two papers and one textbook published. The textbook is currently being used by over five hundred colleges and universities where forensic science is taught."

"Thank you, Dr. Fenton. Your Honor, I would like to submit Dr. Fenton's qualifications and ask that he be certified as an expert witness."

"Defense is acquainted with Dr. Fenton and will so stipulate," Allison said.

"The court will accept Dr. Fenton as an expert witness," Judge Crader ruled.

"Thank you, Your Honor. Dr. Fenton, Dr. Baker took certain scrapings from the wound and submitted these to you for your examination, did he not?"

"He did."

"And what foreign substances, if any, did you find in those wound scrapings?" Stone asked.

"I examined the flakes of rust and determined that the ingredients were composed of iron, zinc, and lead."

"Do these three elements in combination suggest anything to you?"

"Yes. They are consistent with the composition of water-pipe material used in the twenties. I then examined a piece of water pipe taken from the Bristol Victoria Hotel and found that it was composed of the same ingredients, and in the same proportion.''

''Your conclusion then is that the murder weapon was a water pipe?''

''That is what I believe,'' Fenton said. ''Specifically, a piece of water pipe from the remains of the Bristol Victoria Hotel.''

''What other foreign substances did you find?''

''The fibers Dr. Baker spoke of were strands of treated cotton fiber, possibly from a shirt. In addition to the rust and fibers, there was some dirt, lye, and traces of turpentine.''

''Turpentine?''

''Yes.''

''Turpentine such as the kind used by an artist?''

''Yes, I would say so,'' Fenton answered.

''Objection, Your Honor,'' Allison interrupted.

''What is the objection, counselor?'' Judge Crader asked.

''Your Honor, I object to the reference in regard to the turpentine. That is calling for a conclusion on the part of Dr. Fenton.''

''Your Honor, Dr. Fenton has already been certified as an expert witness, and is certainly qualified to identify turpentine,'' Stone protested.

''It isn't the identification of the turpentine I

am challenging, Your Honor. It is Dr. Fenton's suggestion that the turpentine is the kind used by artists. As far as I know, Dr. Fenton is not an artist, and if so, his expert qualifications do not extend to the field of art, and therefore he cannot make the assumption that the turpentine is of the kind used by an artist.''

''Your Honor, artists use brushes, paint, canvas, and turpentine,'' Stone said. ''Baseball players use balls, bats, and gloves. What kind of qualification do you need to state the obvious?''

''Your Honor, my nephew plays Little League baseball,'' Allison said. ''He uses an aluminum bat. I mentioned a few moments ago that I enjoy watching the Yankees play, but I've never seen any of them use an aluminum bat.''

''Aluminum bats aren't used in the majors,'' Stone explained.

Allison smiled broadly. ''Thank you, counselor, you've made my point,'' she said. ''The obvious is *not* always what it seems.''

''Objection sustained. Jury will disregard the reference.''

''Your Honor, I'm confused now. What is the jury being asked to disregard? The fact that turpentine was found in the wound, or just that artists use turpentine to clean their brushes and thin their paint?'' Stone asked.

''Mr. Stone,'' the judge cautioned.

"I'm sorry, Your Honor," Stone said. "I am merely asking for clarification."

"The fact that turpentine was found in the wound may be used," Crader said. "Any speculation as to what the turpentine might have been used for, cannot."

"Thank you," Stone said. He turned to Dr. Baker again. "Just so it hasn't been lost in the shuffle, would you say again, please, the foreign substances you found in the wound."

"Oxide of iron, zinc, and lead; dirt, a few cotton fibers, lye, and some traces of turpentine," Fenton said.

"Thank you, Dr. Fenton. Your witness, Miss McKenzie."

"Dr. Fenton, did you find any traces of oil paint in the wound?"

"No."

"Did you find anything else that painters commonly use? Linseed oil? Brush fibers? Acetate fixative?"

"Objection, Your Honor," Stone said.

"On what grounds?"

"Prosecution objects to the words 'anything else that painters commonly use,' on the same grounds that Defense objected to our use of the words 'turpentine as normally used by an artist.' It would seem to me that the same ground rules apply here."

"I agree, counselor," Judge Crader said.

"Objection sustained. Jury will disregard the words 'anything else that painters commonly use.'"

"Very well, Dr. Baker, I will restate my question," Allison said. "Did you find linseed oil?"

"No."

"Brush fibers?"

"No."

"Acetate fixative?"

"No."

"Thank you, Dr. Fenton. No further questions."

"Redirect, Mr. Stone?" Judge Crader asked.

"No, Your Honor."

"Then, before you call your next witness, I think that, due to the lateness of the hour, I shall call a halt to the proceedings until nine o'clock tomorrow morning," Judge Crader said. He turned to the jury box. "Ladies and gentlemen of the jury, you are reminded not to discuss this case among yourselves, or with anyone else." Crader brought down his gavel. "Court is recessed until nine o'clock tomorrow morning."

Chapter Eight

Superior Court, the Next Day

"**Y**our Honor, the state calls Dr. T. J. Fullman to the stand," Stone said.

Dr. Fullman, wearing brown slacks, a
brown tweed jacket, and a tan sweater vest, was
sworn in and seated on the witness stand. He
took his glasses off and began to polish them as
Stone approached.

"Are you a medical doctor, Dr. Fullman?"

"Yes," Dr. Fullman replied. "But my practice
is almost entirely psychiatric."

"And, in your capacity as a psychiatrist, you
treated Mary Stillman did you not?"

"Technically, the answer to that would be
no," Dr. Fullman replied.

Dr. Fullman's answer surprised Stone.

"I beg your pardon? You didn't treat Mary Stillman?"

"I spoke with her several times and I recommended, in the strongest possible way, that she be admitted to a psychiatric hospital for treatment, but nothing came of it. Then, as her condition got worse, I saw her less and less, until one day she disappeared completely."

"What, exactly, was her condition, Doctor?"

"I wish I could tell you," Dr. Fullman replied. "If I could understand it, I could write a paper on it. You have to understand that psychiatry is not like physics—there aren't laws of exactness by which everything is measured. There are enough disorders with enough similarities to allow us to group them under general headings: paranoia, schizophrenia, manic-depressive, and so forth, but those are just general headings. The essential feature of Mary Stillman's condition was a disturbance or alteration in the normally integrative functions of identity, memory, and consciousness. In general, that puts her in the category known as hysterical neuroses, dissociative type. But, in fact, she didn't fall under any specific subheading of the dissociative disorder field . . . though she exhibited some of the symptoms of multiple personality disorder, psychogenic fugue, and depersonalization neurosis. I have coined my own term for her condition, but I would have to write a paper and get the condition recognized by the American Psychiatric Society for the term to have any validity.''

''What is your term for her condition, Doctor?''

''Psychogenic mood alteration and withdrawal.''

''In layman's terms, what does that mean?''

''As far as I have been able to determine, Mary Stillman had no particular psychic insult in her background. By that I mean she had never been physically, sexually, or mentally abused as a child, or as a wife. She was not an alcoholic, nor did she use drugs. And there is no record of any injury that could have caused the onset of her condition. Despite that, sometime in her late twenties Mary began to be distracted, spending long periods of time totally disassociated with what was going on around her . . . with reality, in other words. If you talked to her, it was as if she didn't even hear you. Her mother and her brother, her husband, even her daughter, became strangers to her as she began, more and more, to withdraw into her own world. Finally it reached the point to where that private world which was occupied by her psyche became so incompatible with the world in which she found herself, physically, that she had to leave.''

''That's when she went out on the streets?''

"Yes."

"When these symptoms first presented themselves, why wasn't she committed to a hospital?"

"The family didn't want to do that."

"You were her doctor. Could you have gotten a court order that would override the family?"

"Perhaps, but you have to consider the times," Dr. Fullman replied. "Do you remember the sixties? Timothy O'Leary, 'Drop out, turn on, and tune in.' This was the time of flower children, hippies and communes. It would have been extremely difficult in those days to get a court order to commit one person to a mental hospital for doing what countless thousands of others were doing all across the country."

"But Mary wasn't just living the life of a hippie, was she, Doctor?"

"No, her condition coincided with the times, but I don't believe it had anything to do with the times. And, of course, many of yesterday's hippies and flower children are today's Wall Street brokers."

"But Mary's condition never changed?"

"No. The others came in from the street. Mary stayed."

"Doctor, it has to be tough to live on the streets. How could someone of Mary's decreased capacity cope well enough to survive out there? I mean, she obviously couldn't cope with what was—physically, at least—a very comfortable environment in her own home.''

"I did not see Mary again, once she became a permanent street person. But, typically, there would be a compensatory adjustment of her skills,'' Dr. Fullman said. "The normal societal skills of a woman her age and standing were useless to her. She no longer needed to know how to drive a car, select a wardrobe, serve tea, make witty, social conversation, host parties, or anything like that. As a result, those skills atrophied, to be replaced by skills that she could use . . . where to find food, shelter, and warmth.''

"There are other skills a street person needs, are there not, Doctor? For example, we know that there are people who prey upon the helpless and the indigent. Would you say that the ability to avoid such people would be one of the compensatory skills Mary would have to develop?''

"Objection, calls for a conclusion.''

"Your Honor, Dr. Fullman is testifying as an expert witness in this field. Indeed, in the area of Mary Stillman's mental condition, he is, perhaps, the only expert. I suggest, therefore, that his conclusion is acceptable evidence.''

"Overruled. You may answer the question, Doctor.''

"Your question was, do I think Mary Stillman

developed the skill of recognizing people who might be dangerous to her, and learned how to avoid them?"

"Yes."

"I believe that would be one of the compensatory skills she would have developed, yes," Dr. Fullman said.

"Then anyone who got close enough to her to bludgeon her to death would have to be known by her? Like a brother, perhaps?"

"Objection, Your Honor."

"Sustained. Mr. Stone, you know better than to ask such a question," Judge Crader scolded.

"I apologize, Your Honor," Stone said, sitting down. "Your witness, counselor."

Allison walked over to Dr. Fullman, smiling warmly at him before she began her questioning.

"Dr. Fullman, over the course of your examination and observation of Mrs. Stillman's condition, did you have the occasion to talk to other members of her family?"

"Yes, of course."

"With whom did you speak?"

"Her husband, her brother, and, of course, her mother, before her mother died."

"What was the attitude of her family toward her?"

"They were worried about her."

"Did you ever observe anything that might

lead you to believe that any of them may have contributed, in part, to Mary's condition?"

"No, I did not."

"Did you ever doubt any family member's love or concern for Mary?"

"No, I did not."

"Now, Dr. Fullman, for just a moment I want you to disregard all the evidence and the testimony that might be presented in this case. Let's say you weren't even here to see and hear what was going on. Let's say you were on vacation in Hong Kong or some such place, and you just happened to read in the newspapers that Byron McCready has been found guilty of the murder of his sister. Based upon what you know of Byron McCready, would you be surprised?"

"Objection!" Stone barked.

"Your Honor, I didn't introduce this witness's expertise in the field of drawing conclusions about a person's behavior, Mr. Stone did. I suggest that if he can draw a conclusion as to how Mary Stillman might act based solely upon observations that he made nearly thirty years ago, he should certainly be able to draw a conclusion as to how Byron McCready might act. I might add that I have no prior knowledge as to what Dr. Fullman's answer to my question will be. It might even be damaging to my client's case, but I would like to hear it."

"Objection overruled," Judge Crader said. "Witness may answer."

"I would be very surprised," Dr. Fullman said.

"Why is that?"

"It doesn't fit Byron McCready's psychological profile. This was a particularly violent murder, with the killer using a club to bash in the victim's head. When someone like Byron McCready kills another person, it is generally in a more impersonal way . . . with poison, or at the very least, a gun."

"Thank you, Doctor. No further questions."

Stone stood up. "Dr. Fullman, you are not suggesting that McCready is psychologically incapable of murder, are you?"

"No, I'm not saying that. I'm just saying that I have a difficult time imagining Byron McCready committing a murder in this fashion."

"Dr. Fullman, have you made a psychiatric examination of Byron McCready?"

"No, I have not."

"But before Mary left, you did examine her?"

"Yes. As I said, that was many years ago, but yes."

"Therefore, when you come to a conclusion on Mary's behavior, it has some basis in clinical observation?"

"That is true."

"Whereas, the answer you just gave the defense counselor is based upon, what? Intuition?''

''Intuition, yes, I would say that would be a fair judgment.''

''Dr. Fullman, would you give that intuition the same weight as an observation you might make after extensive examination? In other words, would you stake your professional reputation on your intuition if you had no empirical evidence to back it up?''

''No, I would not.''

''Thank you, Doctor. Your Honor, the state would now like to call Sister Theresa Margaret Todaro.''

Sister Theresa took the stand, then testified as to seeing Mary talking in an animated fashion with some man on the night before she was found murdered. The man Sister Theresa saw Mary with was Byron McCready. Robinette handled the questioning, then turned his witness over to Allison McKenzie.

Allison greeted Sister Theresa with a warm, disarming smile.

''I'm sorry you had to come down here and participate in this, Sister. It must be rather distressing for you,'' she said.

''No, not particularly,'' Sister said. ''In fact, I confess to finding the whole thing rather fascinating. And I feel as I am doing my public duty.''

"Good, good, that is exactly the way you should feel, Sister. Now, you have been introduced as a witness for the prosecution, but that doesn't necessarily make us adversaries. In fact, I consider myself in partnership with Mr. Stone and Mr. Robinette, with the judge and the jury, and with the people of New York. You see, Sister, what all of us want, prosecution and defense alike, is the truth. 'Seek the truth, and it shall make you free.' We don't challenge the fact that you saw Byron McCready in conversation with his sister. In fact, when Mr. McCready takes the stand in his own behalf, later, he will testify that he did, indeed, meet with his sister that evening, in front of the Redemption House kitchen. But let me ask you this. Did you see them leave together, Sister?"

"No, I did not."

"Did you see Mr. McCready strike his sister, or, in any way, do her harm?"

"No, I did not."

"You said you saw them talking animatedly. Could you hear what they were talking about?"

"No, I could not."

"So, in our search for truth, Sister, the only thing you can actually offer, and to which we agree, is that Mr. McCready did talk to his sister on the night she was killed."

"Yes."

"Thank you, Sister. No further questions."

"Does Prosecution wish to redirect?"

"No, Your Honor," Stone said. "Prosecution wishes to call Miss Lucy Ball."

Lucy made a totally different appearance from the woman Cerreta and Logan had interviewed when they encountered her in the old Avery Building. She was wearing a new dress, her hair was done, and she had even put on a little makeup.

In questioning, it was established that Miss Ball's only source of income was from whatever "odd jobs" she could do for pedestrians on the street. She admitted that she got more money from "the generosity of others" than she did from any such work actually performed.

"Where do you live, Miss Ball?" Stone asked.

"I've got a room up on Fifty-third," she said. "I don't exactly know the address."

"Were you recently a resident of the Avery Building?"

"Yes."

"And while there, did you know Mary Stillman?"

"I didn't know her last name," Lucy said. "I knew her as Queen Mary."

"Were you and Mary friends?"

"Not exactly," Lucy replied. "She didn't have any friends."

"You say she didn't have any friends. Do you

think she might have angered someone?" Stone asked.

"Angered who?"

"Anyone. Can you think of any reason why one of the indigent people who lived in the Avery Building, or who hung out around that area, might have wanted to do her harm?"

"Are you asking me if I think one of us did her in?"

"Yes, I suppose I am."

"I sure didn't."

"Not you, specifically."

"But one of us, right?" Lucy asked. "One of us indigents?"

"Yes."

Lucy shook her head. "No, I don't think so."

"Why not?"

"Queen Mary didn't have any friends . . . she didn't have any enemies. She lived her life all alone, you know what I mean? She didn't talk to any of us, but she didn't bother any of us either. None of us talked to her, and none of us bothered her. And none of us killed her."

"In the statement you gave the police, you said you saw her last at just after eight o'clock on the evening of the night she was killed. Has anything happened to cause you to reconsider that statement?"

"No," Lucy said. "The statement is right. I saw her last at just after eight."

"Thank you. Your witness."

"Miss Ball," Allison said. "When you saw Mary at eight o'clock that evening, was Mr. McCready with her?"

"No," Lucy said.

"Was anyone with her?"

"No."

"Sister Theresa stated that she saw Mary speaking with Mr. McCready just in front of the Redemption House kitchen at shortly after seven that evening. Did you see her then?"

"No."

"Did you, at any time, see Mr. McCready with Mary Stillman?"

"No."

"Thank you, no further questions."

"No redirect, Your Honor. Prosecution now calls Bertis Grisham to the stand."

"Call the witness, bailiff," Judge Crader instructed.

Bertis Grisham was sworn in as a witness for the prosecution. He was wearing blue jeans, a tan jacket, a red plaid shirt, and a blue-and-white striped tie. His long hair was combed straight back, and his beard was clipped short.

"Mr. Grisham, what is your occupation?" Stone asked.

"I'm a burger-doodle cook," Grisham replied.

"Burger-doodle? Is that a chain?"

"No, it's just a word I use that means any fast-food burger place," Grisham said. "You know, McDonald's, Burger King, Wendy's, places like that."

"Which one do you work for?"

"I don't work for any particular restaurant at any particular time," Grisham said. "You see, the turnover is so great that on any given day I can go to any of them and get a job. So what I do is work for a while, then quit so I can do other things, then, when the money runs out, go to work again."

"You say you do other things. What other things do you do?"

"I demonstrate," Grisham said. "I believe that I have a mission in life, and my mission is to call attention to injustice."

"And have you been demonstrating at the site of the new Stillman Towers construction?"

"Yes."

"Mr. Grisham, did you know Mary Stillman?"

"I knew her as Queen Mary."

"Did you know her well enough to have conversations with her?"

"Yes."

"And were you ever in her room?"

"Yes, on several occasions."

"Would you consider yourself her friend?"

"Yes, I would say so," Grisham replied. "I know that the previous witness said she was not particularly friendly with any of the other street people, but I believe that was because she saw them as a threat. I think she respected what I was trying to do, not only for her, but for all humanity."

"When was the last time you saw Mary Mc-Cready?"

"I saw her on the evening of the twenty-first of September."

"Did you see anyone with her?"

"No."

"Now, Mr. Grisham, I ask you to look at the defendant, Mr. McCready, and tell the court if you have ever seen him before?"

"Yes."

"Where did you see him?"

"I saw him going into the Avery Building."

"The Avery Building. That would be the building where Mary had her room?"

"Yes."

"What time was that?"

"That was just after eight o'clock."

"What makes you so certain of the time?"

Grisham smiled. "Because fifteen minutes later I was arrested for disturbing the flow of traffic."

"Thank you, Mr. Grisham. Your witness, counselor."

Allison conferred for a few moments with her client before she stood up.

"Mr. Grisham, though I have questioned the specific details of all the testimony given before now, I haven't questioned the witnesses' veracity. Now, however, I feel that I must. You see, the testimony you have just given is in direct conflict with the statement given by Mr. McCready, and with testimony he will himself give when he takes the stand in his own behalf. Will you explore those differences with me?"

"Okay," Grisham replied.

"The way I see it, there are three possible explanations to account for these differences," Allison said. She held up three fingers on her left hand, then enumerated them with her right as she made her points.

"One, you have made an honest mistake and you have misidentified the person you saw going into the Avery Building. Could that be possible, Mr. Grisham?"

Grisham shook his head, no. "It was McCready," he said.

"All right, then, the second possibility is that you have made an honest mistake on the time. Mr. McCready has admitted in his statement, and will say from the witness stand, that he did go into the Avery Building, though it was much earlier than you claim. He says that it was a little after six. Could that be possible, Mr. Grisham?"

Again Grisham shook his head no. "It was just after eight o'clock," he said.

"Well, then, Mr. Grisham, that only leaves one possibility," Allison said. "Either you, or Mr. McCready, is lying, and the jury is going to have to sort out which of you that would be. Do you have anyone who can corroborate your claim to have seen Mr. McCready enter the Avery Building at a little after eight?"

"No," Grisham said. "I didn't point it out to anyone. I didn't know, at the time, that it would be significant."

"Thank you, Mr. Grisham. I have no further questions."

"Your Honor, Prosecution rests its case," Stone said.

"Very well," Judge Crader replied. "Miss McKenzie, you may begin your case."

"Your Honor, at this time Defense would like to present a motion for a directed verdict."

"Overruled," Judge Crader replied. "Please proceed with your case, Miss McKenzie."

"Thank you, Your Honor. Defense would like to call Mr. Greg Williams to the stand."

Greg Williams was tall, thin, and totally bald. He took the oath then sat down and looked out over the crowded courtroom.

"Mr. Williams, what is your occupation, sir?" Allison asked.

"I own an artists' supply shop," Williams said. "I also do a little dealing in art, generally in works by the lesser-known artists."

"And do you know the defendant, Byron Mc-Cready?"

"Oh, yes, I've known Mr. McCready for many years," Williams replied.

"What is the basis of your relationship with Mr. McCready?"

"He patronizes my shop," Williams said. "I furnish him with all his art materials; paint, brushes, canvas, and so forth. He has also graciously agreed to allow me to handle a small portion of his work. I'm very pleased with that, because the quality of his work is such that it has a tendency to enhance the value of the other pieces I handle."

"Now, Mr. Williams, when it comes to the materials one needs to paint, would you say you are Byron McCready's exclusive supplier?"

"Yes, I'm sure I am. Mr. McCready is very particular about some things, and I go to great lengths to see that he is pleased."

"Would one of the things he is particular about be the kind of brush cleaner and paint thinner he uses?"

"Yes, especially that, brush cleaner and paint thinner."

"We heard yesterday that all artists use turpentine as a brush cleaner. Is that so?"

"It is partially true," Williams replied. "Some artists use turpentine exclusively, other use turpentine and linseed oil. Mr. McCready, in fact, uses a blend of turpentine and linseed oil. Not separately, mind you, but blended together. And the blending has to be just so. If it is off only slightly—for example, if there is too much turpentine or too much linseed oil—he will refuse it. It took me four of five orders before I finally got the blend just right. In fact, I won't let anyone else in my shop prepare the blend but me."

"If Mr. McCready was painting and he ran out of that special blend, would he use pure turpentine?"

Williams shook his head. "Absolutely not," he said. "You or I might not notice the difference in the texture and tint of the paint, thinned by pure turpentine, but Mr. McCready would. That's what makes him an artist . . . and I," Williams sighed, "someone who can only sell to artists."

"Thank you, Mr. Williams. Your witness."

Stone stood up, but he didn't leave his table. "Mr. Williams, in this blend you concoct for Mr. McCready, which is the dominant substance, turpentine or linseed oil?"

"Turpentine."

"Thank you," Stone said, sitting down again.

"Your Honor, defense calls Byron McCready to the stand," Allison said.

Byron McCready stood up, adjusted his tie

nervously, then walked over to the witness stand.

"Raise your right hand."

McCready did so.

"Do you swear to tell the truth, the whole truth, and nothing but the truth, so help you God?"

"I do."

"Be seated."

McCready took his seat.

"Byron, let's get this out of the way right at the offset," Allison said. "Did you kill your sister?"

"No, I did not."

"But you did see your sister on the night she was killed, did you not?"

"Yes."

"And she did come to your apartment before that?"

"Yes," McCready admitted.

"When the detectives came to talk to you about your sister, why did you tell them you hadn't seen her for many years?"

"I was afraid," McCready said. "They told me she was dead, that she had been murdered. I mean, I hadn't seen her in all those years, then she suddenly reappeared in my life. I saw her twice, then she was murdered. All those years she was out on the street and nothing happened to her . . . then this. I didn't know what to do."

"Why did she come to see you?"

"She wanted me to go to Arthur, to talk him out of destroying the Avery Building."

"And what did you say to her?"

"I tried to talk her into coming in off the street. I told her that we loved her and we wanted to take care of her. I begged her to let me get her into a hospital."

"What was her answer to that?"

"She told me that I had no right to tell her how to live her life. And she begged me again to stop the destruction of the Avery Building. She even reminded me that it was the last building that still had our maternal grandfather's name. She said that the building had been left to her . . . and no one had the right to destroy it. She said Arthur stole it from her by manipulating the taxes.

"I told her she was being foolish, that Arthur had every right to do with the building as he saw fit, since she had, in effect, left it to him. I told her also that she couldn't have it both ways. If she wanted to live on the street like a dog, then she would just have to take what the street had to offer. If she wanted more, then she should come in and seek help."

"But she didn't take your advice?"

"No, she did not."

"What did she do?"

"She reminded me of the money she had in escrow," McCready said. "She offered it all to me if I would talk Arthur out of destroying the Avery Building."

"What did you think about that?"

"I was surprised."

"Surprised that she would make such an offer?"

"I was surprised that she even knew about the account. That was the first time I had seen her since Mother died."

"What did you say to her when she made that offer?"

"I told her I would talk to Arthur."

"And did you talk to Arthur?"

"No."

"Did you have any intention of talking to him?"

"No. I just told her that to calm her down."

"But you did see her again, didn't you?"

"Yes, that same evening, I went down to the Avery Building to look for her."

"And what did you find?"

"The way she was living is almost indescribable. The stench in the place was awful. There were people there who were little more than animals. I asked around—most of them wouldn't even talk to me—but finally I got someone to tell me which room was my sister's. I went there, but she wasn't there."

"What time did you go into her room?"

"It was a little after six."

"You are sure of the time?"

"I'm absolutely certain of the time," Byron said. "I waited for her for about thirty minutes and, during that time, I looked at my watch, frequently. I found the building very . . . frightening, and I didn't want to be in there after it got dark."

"While you were waiting, did you touch anything?"

"There's very little that I didn't touch," McCready answered. "I pulled out drawers, opened doors, looked on the shelves. Compared to everything else I had seen in the building, her room was really quite well-kept. I must confess to a certain rather perverse pride in the fact that, even in her current state, she had apparently not sunk to the level of the others who were living in the building."

"So, you are not surprised that the police found your fingerprints in your sister's room?"

"I would be surprised if they did not find them there."

"Did your sister return to her room while you were there?"

"No. When I finally let myself out, I asked again for her, and someone suggested that she might be taking her dinner at the Redemption House kitchen, so I went over there to look for her.''

''Did you go into Redemption House?''

''No. The smell . . . they were having cabbage, I think, and the odor of it cooking, mixed with the stench of so many unwashed bodies . . . I couldn't bring myself to go in.''

''But you did see your sister?''

''Yes. I waited outside and I saw her as she was leaving.''

''What did you talk to her about?''

''I lied to her. I told her I talked to Arthur and he turned me down. Then I reminded her that if she didn't claim her inheritance within the next month, she would lose it. I asked her to try and remember something of our youth, to try and find at least one warm memory of me, of our time together as children. I told her that if she didn't want the money for herself, then to please claim it and give it to me. If she would do that, I promised, I would find a nice building for her somewhere, buy it, and guarantee her that she could live there, unmolested, for as long as she wanted.''

''And what was her reply?''

''She said that money was the tool of Satan, and she was sorry that it still had its hold on me. She said if she gave me the money, it would only make matters worse.''

"Were you upset?"

"Yes, very."

"What did you do then?"

"Nothing. There was nothing I could do. I just turned and walked away. I never saw her again."

"Mr. McCready, did you go down there alone?" Allison asked.

"No," McCready answered.

"Who went with you?"

"Steven Jensen."

"Who is Steven Jensen."

"Steven is my student . . . my protégé," McCready said. "He is a fine young artist with a great deal of potential. I've taken him under my wing, so to speak."

"And . . . in your bed, Mr. McCready?" Allison asked.

McCready bowed his head and pinched his temples between his thumb and middle finger.

"Mr. McCready?"

"I, uh, have tried to be very discreet about that," he finally said, speaking so quietly that he could barely be heard.

"I see. You have not 'come out' as they say?"

"No."

"But Steven is out, is he not?"

"Yes."

"Are you ashamed of your homosexuality, Mr. McCready?"

"You have to realize that I am from an older, more conservative time," McCready replied. "Steven is younger, more courageous. He has no problem with being gay. He even belongs to one of those gay-pride groups. But it is difficult for me to deal with it."

"And yet here, on the witness chair and under oath, you do admit to being homosexual, do you not?"

"Yes," McCready said.

"And Steven Jensen, in addition to being your protégé, is also your homosexual lover. Is that also true?"

"Yes."

"You say Steven was with you when you went down to talk to your sister. Was he with you from the time you left her, until the next morning?"

"Yes."

"Where did you go?"

"We came back to my apartment."

"Did anyone see you together that evening?"

"Yes."

"And in fact, the next morning for breakfast as well. Isn't that right?"

"Yes."

"Who would that be?"

"My maid, Edna Jackson," McCready replied.

"Thank you, Mr. McCready, I have no further questions," Allison said.

Stone walked over to stand in front of the witness chair. "Mr. McCready, did Mr. Jensen go with you into your sister's room?"

"No. He waited in the car."

"Prior to you going into your sister's room, did Mr. Jensen enter the Avery Building with you?"

"No."

"I believe you said you questioned some of the indigents while you were looking for your sister. Was Mr. Jensen with you during that time?"

"No."

"Was Mr. Jensen with you when you finally found your sister?"

"He was in the car."

"At any time while you were in that area, did anyone see Mr. Jensen with you?"

"Steven never left the car the whole time we were there," McCready said. "The only way anyone could have seen us would be if they saw us together in the car."

"Where was the car parked during this time?"

"It was on the street alongside the curb," McCready said.

"Are there parking places there?"

"No, not really," McCready replied. "But Steven was in the car. If any policemen came along, he was prepared to drive away if need be."

"Did any policemen come along?"

"No."

"In other words, Mr. McCready, we have only yours and Mr. Jensen's word that the two of you were together?"

"My maid saw us together," McCready said.

"She saw you in your apartment that evening, and at breakfast the next morning. That hardly accounts for the whole time, does it?"

"But there's Steven."

"Yes, there is Steven," Stone said. "No further questions, Your Honor."

"Redirect?"

"No, Your Honor. At this time defense would like to call Mr. Steven Jensen to the stand."

At the same moment Allison McKenzie was conducting her redirect of Steven Jensen, Paulie Margolis, the supervisor of the construction site at Stillman Towers, was watching his men remove some damaged wooden forms from an excavation where a concrete base was to have been poured. The concrete was originally scheduled to have been poured nearly two months ago, but it was continually postponed due to one problem or another. Then a rain, followed by a freeze, caused the wooden forms to split. That meant the old forms would have to be removed and new ones put in their place before the concrete job could be completed.

"Careful there, now, careful," Margolis said, as one of the workers connected the crane hook to the chain he had wrapped around the form. "Pull it up slow, men, we don't want it bustin' all to pieces. That happens, we'll have a hell of a time getting it out."

"Don't worry, Paulie, it'll hold," the worker said.

"Yeah? It better. If it don't, I'm goin' to wrap you up in chain and have Tony deposit your ass about seventeen floors up, somewhere," Margolis teased, and the others laughed.

"Okay!" the worker shouted. "Pull it up, Tony! But be careful! Don't jerk it!"

Tony, who was operating the crane, began lifting the concrete forms. The two-by-eight boards creaked and groaned as they came up, but with a man on each end to offer support, they didn't break apart.

"Okay, put it down over there," Margolis ordered. "And let's get the new form down in the hole. I'd like to get the concrete poured sometime this year."

"Hey, Paulie!" one of the men called. "Paulie, come over here. Look at this. What is that down there?"

Margolis walked over to look down into the deep, narrow trench.

"I don't know," he said. "It looks like a piece of water pipe or something, and a rag—" Margolis stopped in mid-sentence. "Sonofabitch," he said. "You know what I think that is?"

"What?"

"You remember that old broad they found dead here a couple of months ago? I think we just found the weapon that killed her. Mike, get on the horn and call the police."

District Attorney's Office, Next Morning

"We're taking a beating, Adam," Stone said. "That's all I can say. We're taking a beating."

"You don't know that," Wentworth replied. "You never know what a jury is going to do."

"Ben's right," Robinette said. "I dread even going in there this morning. The way this thing is going, if I were on the jury, even I would vote for acquittal. We never should have taken it to trial."

"Well, I don't want to say I told you so, but—" Wentworth started.

"But you just did," Stone said with a laugh. "Thanks a lot. I swear, if this was a boxing match, I'd throw in the towel. God, I can just see the summation now."

"Maybe we'll get something out of it," Robinette said. "Maybe she'll come dressed in a bikini."

"No way. Tomorrow she'll look like a junior high school librarian again." Stone sighed. "No, sir. What we need now, gentlemen, is a miracle."

The door to Wentworth's office opened and one of the other assistant D.A.'s stuck her head in. "Ben, or Paul, there's a phone call for either one of you from Detective Cerreta."

Robinette was nearest Wentworth's phone, and he looked toward Wentworth.

"Yeah, sure, go ahead, take it in here if you want to," Wentworth said.

Robinette picked up the phone.

"This is Robinette. What? When? Yes, thank you, Phil. I'll tell Ben. And let us know as soon as you get all the particulars on it, will you?"

"What is it?" Stone asked as Robinette hung up the phone.

"You know the miracle you were looking for?"

"Yes."

Robinette grinned broadly. "It may have just happened. That was Cerreta. They found what they believe was the murder weapon."

"You're kidding me."

"No, I'm not. And it is an iron water pipe, just like Fenton said."

"All right," Stone said, jabbing his fist into the air.

"Where on earth did they find it?" Wentworth asked.

"Whoever killed her dropped it down into a cement form, apparently thinking that the cement would be poured soon and it would be covered up. But the cement wasn't poured and the forms had to be replaced. When they took the old forms out, they found the pipe."

"Where is it now?"

"Fenton has it down at Forensics."

"I'm going to call Judge Crader and ask for a delay until this afternoon," Stone said. "By that time, Forensics should be through with it. Tell me, Adam, is it asking too much to want a good match of McCready's fingerprints?"

"It's definitely the murder weapon," Fenton told Cerreta and Logan. "The composition of the pipe is the same as the composition of the flakes of rust we found in the victim's wound. The blood on the cloth and on the pipe matches the victim's blood. In addition, the cloth matches the cotton fibers found in the victim's wound."

"What about fingerprints?"

"We're lucky there too," Fenton replied. "The pipe was lying under the foundation forms, so the weather and the rain couldn't get to it. I managed to get a really good set of prints."

Half an hour later Logan had two fingerprints on the computer screen. On the right was one of McCready's prints taken from the police files. On the left was the best of the prints taken from the pipe. Using the mouse to manipulate the pictures on the screen, Logan brought the two prints into superimposition.

"Shit," he said. "They don't match."

"Do the others," Cerreta suggested. "One of them has to match."

One by one Logan superimposed the lifted print over McCready's fingerprints. Not one of them matched.

"What the hell?" Cerreta said. "Are you sure those are McCready's prints?"

"I'm positive," Logan said. "We printed him as soon as we booked him."

"They don't match."

"You noticed that, did you?" Logan asked sarcastically.

Cerreta leaned back in his chair and folded his arms across his chest.

"Our friends down at the D.A.'s office aren't going to like this," he said. "This doesn't do a damned thing to help their case."

"Help their case? If you ask me, it blows their case out of the water," Logan replied. "And when you think about it, it doesn't make us look all that good either. After all, we're the one who gave him McCready."

"Yeah, I know."

"Damnit! It has to be McCready," Logan said.

Cerreta shook his head. "No, it doesn't. Come on, Mike, you know better than to get the answer and try to make the facts fit. If the facts don't fit, you don't have the answer. We're going to have to start all over. So, what do you say we compare it with the other prints we found in the vic's room?"

"We can start with what's his name—the demonstrator. I've already got his prints on the computer program."

"Grisham," Cerreta said. "Bertis Grisham. Okay, we may as well. It can't be him, though. He was in jail that night, remember?"

"Yeah, well, let's eliminate him from the search anyway," Logan said as he called up Grisham's prints. He began superimposing the lifted print over Grisham's prints, just as he had with McCready's prints.

"Uh-oh," he said a moment later.

"What is it?"

"We've got a match here," Logan said. "Come around here and take a look."

Cerreta walked around behind the computer monitor and looked at the superimposed prints.

There was not one swirl out of place. It was a textbook match.

"What do we do now, coach?" Logan asked, leaning back with his arms folded across his chest as he studied the monitor. "Grisham was in jail from eight o'clock on the twenty-first to eight on the twenty-second."

"Maybe he did it before he left."

"Uh—uh. We have an eyewitness who saw her after eight, remember?"

"Yeah, Lucy. Well, maybe our man didn't get into jail as early as he claims," Cerreta suggested.

"Why don't we find out?"

"Let's see, that would be the Midtown South Precinct," Cerreta said. "I know a lieutenant over there. I think I'll give him a call."

"We need a break here," Logan said as Cerreta dialed the number.

"Lieutenant Stewart, please," Cerreta said when his call was answered. This is Detective Sergeant Cerreta." There was another pause. "Hello, Pat, this is Phil. Do me a favor, will you? Find out if you had a Bertis Grisham as a house guest in your detention cell on the night of the twenty-first of September. And if you did, what time did he come in, and what time did you let him go? Okay, thanks." He covered the mouthpiece and spoke to Logan. "He's looking it up now."

"If he was there, we're sucking muddy water on this thing," Logan said. He pointed to the screen. "We have a perfect match and no way to make the connection."

"Well, I'll ask you the same thing I ask about McCready. Are you sure those are Grisham's fingerprints?"

"Positive," Logan said. "It's the same card we did on him when he was brought in for throwing the paint. And don't forget, it matched the prints in the room too, remember?"

"Yeah, I remember," Cerreta said, then there was a voice on the phone. "Pat, yeah, I'm here. He definitely was there, huh? What time was he locked up? And he got out when? Listen, there's no chance there is a mistake on this, is there? I mean, they weren't all let out in the middle of the night or something? Yeah, well, I just thought I would ask. Thanks, Pat."

Cerreta hung up the phone and stroked his chin. "I don't give a damn how many of Grisham's prints we have on the murder weapon, we can't use it," he said. "Grisham was booked at eight-fifteen and he didn't get out until just after eight the next morning."

"After eight?" Logan said.

"Eight-oh-seven to be exact."

"Wait a minute, that can't be," Logan said. "We were at the murder site before eight, remember?"

"Yeah, I remember."

"Well, don't you remember the loudmouth who was shouting at us when we got out of the car?"

Cerreta looked up in surprise. "Sonofabitch! It was Grisham!"

"You're damned right it was!"

"But how can that be?"

Logan looked at Grisham's fingerprint card, then he looked up at Cerreta and smiled.

"Now I'm going to ask you the same question you've been asking me. Is your lieutenant friend sure they had the right man?"

Cerreta picked up the phone and began to dial. "Pat, it's Phil again," he said when Stewart came to the phone. "Listen, I'm going to fax over some fingerprints. Compare them with the prints you got from Grisham, will you? Then call me back."

"Want some coffee?" Logan asked when Cerreta hung up.

"Yeah, thanks."

Logan walked over to the service counter and poured two cups of coffee, then brought them over to the two desks. He and Cerreta drank silently for five minutes . . . fifteen . . . half an hour.

"How damn long does it take the people at Midtown South to look at fingerprints?" Logan finally asked in frustration. "Give them a call, Phil, and see what the hell is going on."

"Take it easy, Mike," Cerreta said easily. "Has anyone ever told you you're an A-type personality?"

"It's not like we asked them to check the FBI file, for chrissake," Logan said.

The phone rang and Cerreta grabbed it. "Cerreta . . . You don't say. Yeah, well, thanks Pat. I owe you one on this."

"What is it?" Logan asked.

"The man they had in jail on the night of the twenty-first was Jay Martin, not Bertis Grisham," he said. "For some reason, Martin identified himself as Grisham. Grisham wasn't there at all. That means he no longer has an alibi."

Logan picked up the phone. "He was one of the witnesses. I'll give the court a call and see if he's down there this morning." He made the call, then hung up in disgust. "He was dismissed yesterday afternoon. And get this. He gave the Avery Building as an address. You know damn well that's wrong."

"All right, let's go find the bastard."

There were only two demonstrators across the street from the construction site when Cerreta and Logan arrived, and they weren't doing much demonstrating. Both were sitting on the sidewalk, leaning against the building, wrapped in blankets to keep warm. A FACE-IT sign leaned against the wall beside them.

"We're looking for Bertis Grisham," Cerreta said, showing his badge.

"Never heard of him."

"Sure you have. He's been demonstrating here for three months."

"Wait a minute," one of the demonstrators said. "Is he the one who threw the red paint?"

"Yeah, that's him," Cerreta said.

"What red paint?" the other demonstrator asked.

"It was bad, man, I told you about that, don't you remember," the first demonstrator said. "This dude went in and threw red paint all over the construction workers."

Both young men laughed. "Yeah, yeah, I heard about that," the second said. "That was before I started comin' out here, though."

"That Grisham, man, he was cool as shit."

"Where is this cool piece of shit now?" Logan asked dryly.

"I don't have any idea. Anyhow, he hasn't been around here for quite a while. Most of the others have gone too, and tomorrow we're leavin', so there won't be anyone left."

"Oh, are you fellas giving up?" Logan asked. "What's the matter? Couldn't get the world to stop?"

"We're making a strategic readjustment of

our efforts," the first demonstrator said. "We're leaving this site because most of the people who were living in the Avery Building have found other places to live by now. Part of winning the war is knowing when to abandon one battlefield and go to another."

"Have you got another battlefield picked out?" Cerreta asked.

"Why do you want to know? So you can go over there and bust us before we even get started?"

"Look, if you want to walk naked in front of the Statue of Liberty, that's no sweat off my balls," Logan said. "We're not into busting demonstrators."

"Then what do you want with Grisham?"

"Well, believe me, it doesn't have anything to do with parading without a permit," Logan said. "Now do you know where he is or not?"

"Beats me, man, I don't have any idea."

Logan reached down to grab the young man by the front of his shirt. He lifted him up. "No, man," he said, coming down on the word *man* in mockery of the way the demonstrator had used it. "That doesn't beat the shit out of you," he said. "I'm the one that's going to beat the shit out of you." He drew his fist back.

"No, wait! Wait! He—He's not even part of our group anymore," he said.

"What are you talking about?"

"Grisham split. He got pissed off because he said we weren't forceful enough. He's joined some other cause."

"What cause?"

"I don't know, man, honest."

"That's not a good enough answer," Logan said.

"I don't know what cause he's with now, but I know he's got a place up on Sixty-fifth. Maybe you can find him there. I don't know the address, but it's between Third and Second. It's above a tobacco store."

Logan smiled, though the smile didn't reach his eyes. "Thank you," he said. "That's what I like to see—a cooperative citizen."

"I didn't have any choice, did I? You were going to beat me up."

"Not really," Logan said. "There's no video cameras around. Haven't you heard? Cops only like to perform on camera."

Cerreta and Logan returned to their car, then started toward the location given them by the demonstrator.

"You're going to get your tail in a crack one of these days if you don't stop doing that," Cerreta cautioned.

"Yeah, I know," Logan said. "I should've been a cop fifty years ago. Do you think there ever really was a time when cops used rubber hoses?"

Cerreta laughed. "Missed your calling, did you, Mike?"

They turned onto Sixty-fifth. "There," Logan said. "If the guy was telling us the truth, that's the only tobacco store on the block."

"Let's check it out."

They left the car and stepped into the doorway. Cerreta ran his finger over the mailboxes, then stopped under a name. "Here it is," he said. "Two B."

The two officers went up the stairs to the second-floor hallway. When they reached the door, they stood to either side of it. Logan knocked.

"Mr. Grisham! Mr. Grisham, open the door, please. We're police officers and we would like to talk to you."

Logan knocked again. The knock was much louder this time and the pounding sound echoed all up and down the hallway. The door across the hall opened and a man looked out.

"Are you officers looking for the gentleman who lives in that apartment?" he asked.

"Yes, sir," Cerreta replied. "Do you know where he is?"

"I imagine you will find him at the demonstration."

"The demonstration? Which demonstration would that be?"

"The AIDS Battle Brigade demonstration," the man said. "Mr. Grisham was quite upset when the Metro Atlantic Bank withdrew their support for the Scarlet Heart Research Foundation. They are very close to finding a cure for AIDS, you know, but there are certain people in the world who, for economic or political reasons, don't want a cure."

"Where did you hear that?"

"Why, it's in this circular Mr. Grisham gave me," the man said, handing a sheet of paper through the door.

Logan took the paper and looked at it for a moment, then looked at his watch. "It's on Lexington," he said. "The demonstration should be going on right now."

"Are you going down there to break it up?" the neighbor asked.

"You might say that," Logan growled.

"Why would you do that? Don't the American people have a right to peacefully assemble anymore? Don't answer that. I know why you want to break up the demonstration. It's because the meeting is about AIDS. Mr. Grisham is right, isn't he? The authorities don't want a cure for AIDS."

"Thank you for your help, sir," Cerreta said as they hurried back down the stairs.

When they got back into the car, Cerreta put the red light on top while Logan drove. "You ever heard of this Scarlet Heart outfit?" he asked.

"Yeah, I've heard of them," Logan said. "Right now they're under criminal investigation. It seems they've been collecting all this money for AIDS but they're using only about ten percent of it for legitimate research. They've been skimming off the rest to pay for luxury condos in Florida, new cars, TV sets, vacation trips to Europe.

"Then I don't get it. Why is this AIDS Battle Brigade protesting the bank for stopping its funding? You'd think they'd be protesting the company that's stealing the research money."

"I think they probably believe that any research is better than no research at all. Besides, they're afraid that if any bad press gets out about any research group, it might have an adverse effect on all of them," Logan said.

"Look up there." Cerreta pointed out. "Looks like something is going on."

There were several hundred people gathered on the sidewalk and spilling out into the street in front of the Metro Atlantic Bank. It wasn't until Logan and Cerreta got out of their car they could see what everyone was looking at. Leaning against the front of the bank was a large cross, and on the cross, with very realistic nails and blood coming from his hands and feet, was a man, naked except for a loincloth. A crown of thorns was on his head and real blood was streaked down his face. The sign above his head read: CHRIST HAS AIDS.

"Jesus," Cerreta muttered. "Those sacrilegious bastards."

At the foot of the cross there were a dozen young men, their arms linked together. All were wearing placards around their necks. Some read: I Am Dying of AIDS. The others read: I Am the Brother of All Who Have AIDS.

"There he is," Logan said, pointing to Grisham. As the two officers moved toward Grisham, he glanced up. For a moment there was a look of confusion on his face, but that was quickly replaced by an expression of fright. Suddenly Grisham got up and started to run. Cerreta ran after him.

"Hey!" one of the demonstrators shouted. "Come back! Don't let them bully us!"

Because there were several people crowded around the demonstration area, Grisham found it difficult to get away. He pushed into the crowd, while Cerreta, with his badge hanging on his jacket pocket, plowed through, right behind him. The men and women who had gathered only to see a little street theater suddenly found themselves involved in a police chase, and they shouted in fear and alarm as they scrambled to get out of the way. As the crowd began to move, however, it made it even more difficult for Grisham to run. Finally he broke through the back end of the crowd, and when he did, let out a victorious shout of defiance.

The shout died in his throat, for there, two steps in front of him, with his arms wide open, stood a grinning Logan.

"Gotcha," Logan said.

Chapter Nine

Superior Court, Afternoon of the Same Day

"**M**r. Stone, I believe you have a motion you wish to make?" Judge Crader said as the session was about to get under way.

"I do, Your Honor."

"Make your motion."

Stone stood up and buttoned his jacket. "Your Honor, new evidence and information has just come to light which totally alters this case. Accordingly, the State of New York wishes to withdraw all charges against the defendant, with the recommendation that Mr. McCready be dismissed."

There were several surprised gasps from the audience, then applause and cheers. Judge Crader gaveled the gallery quiet.

"Very well, Mr. Stone, the court accepts your motion. Charges against Byron McCready are hereby dropped. Mr. McCready you are released from custody and are free to go. You have, sir, the profound apologies of the State of New York. Court is adjourned."

Smiling broadly, Allison came over to talk to Stone and Robinette. She put her hands on the front of the table and leaned forward, showing a generous amount of cleavage. Stone had erred in thinking she would play the role of librarian today. Instead she looked more like someone who could turn letters on a game show.

"It's too bad we didn't finish the case, Benjamin," she said. "My summation would have been dynamite."

Stone chuckled. "I'm sure it would have been, counselor. I'm sure it would have been."

Amy Schumacher showed her assignment letter to the desk sergeant. "I would like to speak with Mr. Bertis Grisham, please," she said.

"You his P.D.?"

"Yes."

"Okay," the desk sergeant said, picking up a phone "Go on into Conference Room Three. I'll have him brought to you."

"Thank you," Amy said. She picked up her briefcase and walked down the short corridor to the door marked CONFERENCE ROOM 3—ATTORNEYS ONLY.

The floor of the room was dark, green tile, the walls a lighter shade of green. There were two doors leading into the room, one from the corridor, through which Amy had entered, and the other leading toward the incarceration area. Both doors had small windows which were screened with a very heavy wire mesh. There was a small, gray metal table in the middle of the room, with a chair on either side of the table.

Amy Schumacher had been a member of the Public Defender's staff for a little over a year. It wasn't in her plans to stay much longer. She had volunteered to serve a year in the P.D.'s office, in the belief that the density of the P.D. caseloads would give her the experience in handling criminal cases equivalent to four years in private practice. That experience, she hoped, would enable her to land a very good position with one of the more successful criminal-law firms.

Amy opened her briefcase and took out the folder on Bertis Grisham. She had not even been assigned the case until this morning, and had had time for only one perfunctory perusal of it before she came down to the jail. She knew from experience, however, that it would be at least fifteen minutes, perhaps longer, before the prisoner would be brought to her. That would allow her to use this time to better acquaint herself with the case . . . and with her client.

As soon as she began reading, she knew that this was a rather unusual person. If ever there was such a thing as a professional demonstrator, Bertis Grisham would fill that bill. Apparently he would demonstrate for anything: environment, animal rights, rights for the homeless, gay rights, women's rights . . . Here was something interesting, she thought. He had once been arrested while protesting abortion in front of a health clinic, then two days later was rearrested in front of the same clinic, carrying a right-to-abortion sign. His most recent arrest had taken place at the site of an AIDS Awareness demonstration, though of course that wasn't the reason for his arrest.

When Amy first drew this case, she thought it might be one of her more interesting ones. Most of her previous cases had been in defense of pickpockets, muggers, and burglars. She had also defended a few stickup artists, but this was the first murder case. However, it was beginning to look as if it would be no case at all. Bertis Grisham had given a complete statement to the police, admitting that he killed Mary Stillman. He had waived his rights to an attorney during the confession, and only now had agreed to see one, when it was too late for a lawyer to do anything for him.

"Why did you even bother to call me?" she muttered to herself.

Amy heard footsteps on the other side of the back door and looked up just as the door was opened. A tall, thin, bearded young man, wearing the bright-orange jumpsuit of a prisoner, was shown into the room by a uniformed officer. The movement of the young man's hands and feet was restricted by the manacles he was wearing.

"Go over there and take a seat, Grisham," the uniformed officer said. "That's your lawyer."

"Where's Barkett?" Grisham asked.

"I don't know anyone named Barkett."

"William Barkett. He's supposed to be my lawyer."

"Did you hire him?"

"No," Grisham said. "I don't have any money to hire a lawyer."

"Then this is your lawyer. She was sent by the P.D.'s office."

Grisham shrugged, then shuffled over to the chair and sat down. He rested his arms on the table.

"Mr. Grisham, my name is Amy Schumacher, and I've been assigned to your case," Amy explained.

"You?" Grisham snorted.

"Yes. If you would like, I will see if I can get someone else to take it."

"I want William Barkett," Grisham said. "He's always been my lawyer before."

"When I was given your file at the office, I saw that you had been previously handled by Mr. Barkett. I called him just before I came over here," Amy said. "You must understand that he is one of the attorneys in Hence Fielding's law firm, working directly for Mr. Fielding. He informed me that he had represented you in the past, when you were charged with an act of civil disobedience in a matter in which Mr. Fielding had a personal interest. But Mr. Barkett was quick to point out that he will not be able to represent you in this case. As I said, Mr. Grisham, if you don't want me on the case, I will see if I can get someone else."

"You mean from the P.D.'s office?"

"Yes. Unless you have the funds to hire a lawyer of your own choosing."

"I don't have any money," Grisham said. He ran his hands through his beard, then sighed. "All right, I'll go with you."

"Yes, well, it may all be a moot point now, anyway. According to this, you have given the police a full confession."

"Yeah, that is a fact," Grisham said. He laughed dryly. "So, tell me, Miss Schumacher, just what can you do for me? Like the confession says, I did kill the woman."

"Perhaps it was in a fit of passion or frustration," Amy suggested. "A spur of the moment thing that would tend to mitigate it. For instance, it gives us a defense against premeditation; an element the State has the burden to prove."

"No, I planned to kill her," Grisham said. "From the moment I found out who she really was, I planned it."

"Have you any remorse?"

"None," Grisham said easily.

Amy sighed. "Mr. Grisham, I would like you to tell me about it in your own words."

"It's all in the statement," Grisham said.

"I want to hear the words spoken."

"Whatever turns you on," Grisham said. He then proceeded to tell Amy the details of how he planned and carried out the murder. She shuddered inwardly as she listened to his dispassionate account.

"Mr. Grisham, I am your counselor, and I want to help you," she said. "But we have to develop some . . ." She paused, looking for the phrase. "Some legal theory to keep you from being tried for Murder Two, and alternatively, to reduce to the minimum the likelihood of a jury convicting you of that charge. Something to make sense of all this. Why did you kill her? From everything I can find out about you, you are a man who is passionately involved in helping others. You demonstrate for the rights of people and animals, you care about the environment, why would you do something like this . . . something that is so totally alien to everything you have always stood for?''

"But this isn't alien to what I stand for, don't you understand?'' Grisham asked.

"No, I don't.''

"It's really very simple,'' Grisham said. "Didn't you see how much publicity that killing brought to the plight of the homeless? Especially once it got out that Queen Mary was not only homeless, she was also rich! Newspapers and television stations all over the country have covered this story.''

"And you did this for publicity?'' Amy asked, aghast.

"Yes. Well, no, not like you think,'' Grisham answered. "For myself, I care nothing. I am just the catalyst. I'm talking about the publicity it brought to the situation of the dispossessed. The whole nation's attention was focused upon the wanton destruction of the places the homeless called home.''

"But Mr. Grisham, it didn't stop the destruction of the old buildings,'' Amy said. "That hasn't missed a beat. In fact, I'm told that everyone who once lived in the Avery Building has gone somewhere else.''

Grisham shook his head. "No, no, no! Don't look at the short term. You must look at the end result," he said. "You do remember the protest of the Vietnam War, don't you, Miss Schumacher?''

"The antiwar demonstrations? Well, yes, I suppose I do, though I was quite young then."

"I can remember watching them all on television," Grisham said. "I was too young to join the protest movement." His eyes shone with excitement. "But oh, what a magnificent experience that must have been. Anyway, to make my point, the people who demonstrated against that war were beaten back at every turn. They had high-pressure water hoses turned on them, they were bombarded with tear gas . . . at Kent State they were cut down by gunfire. In the short term you might say they lost every encounter. But in the long term they won their war. Nothing the President or the Congress did ended the war. They alone, through their actions, their disruptions, and the white-heat of public disdain of the war, made the United States pull out of Vietnam!''

"And you equate what you are doing with the war protest movement?''

"Yes, I think so," Grisham said. "We're all

warriors, we need only a cause. My trial will show that.''

"Your trial? Mr. Grisham, what makes you think you are going to have a trial? You have already confessed.''

"I confessed to the act, not the guilt,'' Grisham said.

"That doesn't make sense.''

"Then make sense of it. You're my lawyer. According to the Constitution, I'm entitled to a trial, am I not?''

"You don't want a trial, Mr. Grisham. If this goes to trial, they're going to go for Murder Two. On the other hand, since they have already had one try at conviction on this case, I believe I might be able to cut a deal with them. I think I can get Man One . . . maybe even Man Two. That could take fifteen to twenty years off your sentence.''

"I want a trial.''

"What would you plead?''

"Not guilty.''

"But you have confessed.''

"I told you, I confessed to the act—not to the guilt.''

"And I told you there is no such thing.''

"Then plead not guilty by reason of justifiable homicide,'' Grisham suggested.

"I can't plead that. This case does not come

under any of the provisions of justifiable homicide.''

Without another word, Grisham abruptly stood up. He walked over to the door and knocked on it.

"Mr. Grisham?" Amy said, surprised by Grisham's sudden and unexpected move. "Mr. Grisham, are you leaving now?"

"Yes," Grisham replied. "There's nothing more for us to talk about."

"But we have not yet resolved the issue. How do you want me to plead for you?"

A uniformed officer answered Grisham's knock. Just before he led Grisham away, however, Grisham looked back toward Amy. "I want a trial, Miss Schumacher. And in that trial, I want you to find some way to tell the jury that even though I killed Mary Stillman, I am not guilty."

"I'll, uh, do what I can," Amy responded.

Amy signed out of the jail, then took a taxi to Dumplin's, a restaurant in mid-Manhattan where she was to have lunch with Thad Limbaugh, a senior partner of Sidwell, Potashnick and Limbaugh. Limbaugh was waiting in the foyer for her.

"Am I late?" Amy asked. "I'm sorry. I was with a client."

Limbaugh, a silver-haired, distinguished-looking man, smiled at her.

"Don't apologize, Miss Schumacher," he said. "As a matter of fact, one of the things our firm likes about you is your dedication to work. Besides, we agreed to meet sometime between twelve-thirty and one, and it is only five till one, so you are well within the parameters."

"Aren't you gracious," Amy said with a pleasant smile.

Limbaugh signaled that his guest had arrived, and they were led to a table at the rear of the busy restaurant. The waiter pulled the table out to allow Amy to sit on the bench seat. When she was seated, Limbaugh sat across from her.

"An interesting case?" Limbaugh asked as he picked up the menu.

"I think perhaps strange, more than interesting," Amy replied. "In fact, I'm sure you've probably heard of it."

Limbaugh held up his finger. "I'll have the veal," he said to the hovering waiter. "And a glass of white wine."

"Yes, I'll have the same," Amy replied, handing her oversized menu back to the waiter.

"I've heard of the case, you say?"

"Yes, I'm certain you have. It is the Stillman case."

"Ah, yes, the indigent woman they found murdered, who turned out not to be indigent at all. They tried her brother first, didn't they?"

"Yes," Amy said. "He was defended by Allison McKenzie."

"Brilliantly defended, I have heard," Limbaugh said. "Did you know that we tried to recruit her for our firm? As you can see, she got away, I'm sorry to say." Limbaugh smiled. "You might be interested to know, however, that one of the reports we have on you, compared you to Allison."

"Really? I'm very complimented by the comparison," Amy said.

"Yes, well, maybe someday Allison McKenzie will be equally complimented to think that she is being compared to you," Limbaugh suggested.

"You aren't only gracious, you are most flattering," Amy said.

"Tell me about your case."

Over veal, Amy discussed her meeting that morning with Bertis Grisham. Limbaugh listened carefully, asking a few questions for clarification here and there, and commenting when he thought a comment was needed.

"Despite his insistence that we go to trial, I don't really see a case for him," Amy concluded.

"What do you mean?"

"The best thing I can possibly do for him is go to the D.A. and try to deal. Hopefully, the fact that they have gone through one trial in this case will make them generous.''

"Amy, I'm disappointed with you,'' Limbaugh said as he sipped his after-lunch cappuccino. "Where is your spirit of adventure . . . your willingness to accept a challenge?''

Amy frowned in confusion. "I beg your pardon?''

"Do you not see the opportunity this case presents you?'' he asked.

Amy shook her head. "No,'' she said. "I don't.''

Limbaugh set his cup down, then dabbed at his lips with his napkin.

"You've nothing to lose with this case, my dear,'' he said. "If you plead him not guilty and the decision goes against you, well, everyone will know that you were up against impossible odds to begin with. But if, against all odds, you make a spirited defense, it would be a wonderful showcase for your skills and talent. When you think about it, you wouldn't even have to win. All you would have to do is make a fight of it. Give the jury something to actually think about.''

"But is that best for the client?''

"Of course it is. Everyone is entitled to a defense.''

"I don't know, Mr. Limbaugh,'' Amy said.

"The only possible defense would be not guilty by reason of insanity."

Limbaugh put his gold card on the tray with the bill, and the waiter took it and withdrew.

"Yes, I'm sure you are right."

"And such a plea is almost always rejected."

"Yes, that is true as well. But what can one do, except play the cards that have been dealt?"

"Like the song says, you should know when to hold them and when to fold them."

"Well of course, the final decision is yours," Limbaugh said. "I'm just suggesting that it would be much easier for me to sell you to the other partners in the firm if you could bring a little attention to yourself with a case like this."

"I would like nothing better than to join your firm," Amy said. "But my first obligation is to my client."

"Yes, we both agree on that," Limbaugh said. "But what am I asking you to do, except give your client your best effort?"

Amy was silent for a long moment, then she smiled. "Actually, that's right, isn't it? There is certainly nothing here that is unethical, or incompatible with Mr. Grisham's best interest. All right, Mr. Limbaugh, I'll plead him not guilty."

Limbaugh signed the credit slip, then looked up at Amy. "Do well, my dear," he said. "We'll be keeping our eyes on you. And, when this case is completed, come see us."

"Thank you, Mr. Limbaugh, for the meal and the advice," Amy said, pushing back the feeling that, somehow, she had just sold her soul.

When Beth Hamilton, Amy's office partner, came into the office that afternoon, she saw Amy sitting at her desk with half a dozen law books open around her. She was copying notes from one onto a yellow legal pad.

"Aren't you the busy beaver, though?" Beth asked, sitting at the desk that butted up against Amy's.

"How did your speech to the Women's Betterment League go?" Amy asked.

"Oh, splendidly," Beth said. "They want me to run for a seat in the state legislature."

"How exciting!"

Beth shook her head. "How boring," you mean. She took off her coat and hung it on the rack, then sat down at her desk, which was just across from Amy's. "New case?" she asked as she started looking through her in-file.

"Yes," Amy said. "You may have read about it. You remember the indigent woman whose body was found at the site of the Stillman Towers construction? The one who turned out to be Stillman's estranged wife?"

Beth stopped sorting for a moment, then looked up at Amy.

"Yes," she said, very quietly. "What about it?"

"Well, I'm defending the man who killed her."

"You mean the man who is accused of killing her," Beth corrected.

"No, not just accused. He killed her. He has already signed a confession."

"Then what is there to defend? Go to the D.A. and cut your best deal."

"Yeah," Amy said. "That's what I planned to do. Until lunch."

"What happened at lunch?"

"I met with Thad Limbaugh. You remember, I told you he's a senior partner in the firm I want to join?"

"Yes, I remember."

"Well, Mr. Limbaugh thinks I should defend Grisham," Amy said. "He believes a good defense will help me get on with them. I mean, I don't even have to win or anything. All I have to do is present a good defense."

"Thad Limbaugh is a pompous ass," Beth said. "Tell him to take his defense and shove it. You don't need him, and you don't need to make a fool out of yourself pleading a case that you can't even dent."

"That's easy for you to say," Amy said. "You're married to the fair-haired prince of Wall Street. To you, playing law is a hobby. I need to try and make a living out of it."

"It is much more than a hobby for me," Beth insisted.

Amy smiled. "I'm sorry, Beth. I didn't mean that the way it sounds. I just meant you don't need the income from this job."

"That doesn't make me any less a lawyer," Beth replied.

"No, of course it doesn't. I know that you're deeply committed to what you do, and I know that your clients wouldn't get any better service from the most expensive firm in the city. In fact, I wish I could call on some of your skill. I wish you could give me some idea as to how I might approach this case."

Beth drummed her fingers on the desk for a moment. "That wouldn't be a very good idea," she finally said. "At least, not for this case."

"Why not? Do you think it would be unethical of me to seek advice on a case that is so important to my future career?"

"No, it isn't that," Beth said.

"Well, what is it, then?"

"It's just . . . this case . . . it isn't very clean," she said. "Like I said, what you should do is go to the D.A. and make your best deal."

"I know. I wish I had any other case in our whole office to defend," Amy said. "But it's too late now. Mr. Limbaugh knows I have this case, and this is the one he's going to be watching. Oh, Beth, please help me. If there's anyone who could come up with an idea as to how to handle it, it would be you.''

''That's not the only thing,'' Beth said. ''I'm just not sure this slime-bucket deserves to be defended.''

''Beth! I've never heard you talk like that about anyone. And we've defended some pretty lowlife people before—rapists, child molesters, and the like. At least Grisham had a purpose for his act. His purpose was perverted because his logic is perverted, but there was a purpose. In his own, insane way, he thought he would be doing good by killing Mary Stillman.''

''Is that what you're going to plead? Insanity?'' Beth asked.

Amy sighed. ''Yes,'' she said. ''If I can get a handle on the approach.''

''Let me see his file,'' Beth asked.

Amy slid the file folder over to her, then sat quietly for the next several minutes while Beth read it. Finally she shut the folder and pushed it back across to Amy.

''There is a way to defend it,'' she said.

''There is? Oh, Beth, would you help me with this case?''

''I can't,'' Beth said. ''Besides, if you want to impress Sidwell, Potashnick and Limbaugh, you're going to have to do all this yourself.''

''Do what? Beth, I don't have the slightest idea of how to approach it. I mean, you said there's a way. Are you just saying that? Or do you really believe there's a way?''

"Yes, there is a way.''

"Then why won't you help me? Where is this commitment you have to the rights of the accused to get the best defense possible?''

"Amy, you don't know what you're asking,'' Beth said. "Don't you understand?''

"Is it because if I'm successful, I'll get all the credit?''

Beth continued to shake her head no.

"All right,'' Amy said quietly. "You evidently have your reasons. I don't know what they are, but I'll respect them. I won't ask you again.''

Beth was silent for a long moment, then sighed. "All right,'' she said. "I'll help you in any way I can. I don't know why I'm doing it, but I'll do it.''

"Thanks, Beth,'' Amy said. "You don't know how much I appreciate this.''

"You don't know how much you should appreciate it,'' Beth replied.

Chapter Ten

District Attorney's Office

"It's a whole new ball game, Ben," Wentworth said. "Now the physical evidence is only secondary to your case, because Grisham is admitting to everything.

"He's entering a plea of guilty?"

Wentworth shook his head. "Defense is entering a plea of not guilty, by reason of insanity."

"Come on, Adam, give me a break," Stone said. "Not guilty by reason of insanity? That is absolutely ridiculous."

"Good, I'm glad you feel that way," Wentworth said. "Now, all you have to do is convince the jury to see it our way."

"Do you have any reason to suspect that the jury might not see it our way?" Robinette asked.

"No," Wentworth replied. "But I've heard that Thad Limbaugh has his eyes on the young P.D. who's going to handle the case. She'll be looking to make an impression."

"How is she going to make an impression by putting up a lead balloon like this?" Stone asked. "There's no way they can make that fly."

"You think not?" Wentworth replied. "Well, I wish I could share your optimism, but what I see is all the talk about this being 'the year of the woman.' And they say Amy Schumacher is another Allison McKenzie. You *do* remember Allison McKenzie, don't you?"

"We were trying to forget. Thanks for reminding us," Robinette said sarcastically.

Wentworth chuckled. "Don't thank me, fellas, that's what I get paid for. I just want you guys to be on your toes with this one, that's all. After losing our first trial, we're now fourth and long and we can't punt, if you get my analogy."

"Maybe we can punt," Stone said. "What if we offer to deal?"

"I'm not prepared to offer anything any better than Man One, and I don't think they'll go for it."

"How about Man Two, with time?" Stone suggested. "It'll save us going through another trial."

Wentworth stroked his chin for a moment, then nodded. "All right, see what you can do. I really would like to get this over with. I don't want this case to become our life's work."

Paul Robinette stood just inside the door looking around the Public Defender's office. It reminded him somewhat of the D.A.'s office, not in its physical layout, for it was much smaller and more crowded, but rather in the kinetic energy of the place. There was the same sense of disorder, for example, the bulletin board so cluttered that urgent messages were pinned on top of other urgent messages. And, as in his own office, the phones were ringing constantly.

"Yes, can I help you?" a young black man asked.

"I'm Paul Robinette from—"

"The D.A.'s office," the young black man said, smiling broadly and extending his hand. "Yes, sir, Mr. Robinette, I know all about you. You were one of my role models while I was in school."

"Really?" Robinette replied. The suggestion surprised him. He hadn't thought himself old enough to be a role model. "Well, I'm . . . flattered." He couldn't think of anything else to say.

"What brings you to the humble P.D. office, Mr. Robinette?"

"I'm here to see Miss Schumacher."

"She shares an office with Mrs. Hamilton,"

the young man said, pointing to the back of the room. "That door. Just go on in, we don't stand much on formality around here."

"Thank you."

Despite the young man's suggestion that he just go in, Robinette knocked on the door. A woman called out to him.

"Yes, come in."

There were two women in the office, one sitting behind one of the desks, and another—only a little older, Robinette guessed—leaning over her, pointing out something in an open book. There were precedents and legal books scattered all over both desks, many of them open to marked pages.

"Miss Schumacher?" Robinette asked.

"I'm Amy Schumacher, what can I do for you?" the seated woman replied.

"I'm Paul Robinette from the District Attorney's office. I would like to talk to you about the Bertis Grisham case."

"Mr. Robinette! Well, well, I am impressed," Amy said. "It isn't often that one of the D.A.'s people come down here to see us. Most of the time we have to go see them, hat in hand. Uh, this is Beth Hamilton. She'll be helping me in the Grisham case."

"Oh?" Robinette replied.

"I won't be in the courtroom," Beth said

quickly. "I'll just be assisting Amy with the re-search."

"And the planning," Amy said. "Let's give credit where credit is due. Now, Mr. Robinette, may I ask the purpose of your visit? Surely you aren't spying in the enemy camp?" she added.

"No, no," Robinette answered, holding up his hands. Then he saw that she was joking. "I guess you caught me on that one," he added sheepishly. "But let me get down to business, Miss Schumacher. As you no doubt know, we have just come through one lengthy trial on this case—"

"And lost it," Amy interrupted.

"Yes, and lost it," Robinette admitted. "And, because of that, we are willing to make you an offer that . . . to be honest with you, we would never even consider under normal circum-stances."

"And what would that offer be?" Amy asked.

"Man Two with time."

"That's a good offer," Beth said.

"Where would the time be served?" Amy asked.

Robinette looked at her as if he didn't under-stand the question. "Why, in prison, of course," he replied. "Where else would it be served?"

"In a hospital where he could get psychiatric help . . . with the provision that he be released as soon as a psychiatric board certifies him cured.''

''As I understand it, Miss Schumacher, that's going to be the thrust of your case,'' Robinette said. ''What you're asking for is for the D.A. to give you a directed verdict, without even bothering to go to trial.''

''Mr. Robinette, you're the one who doesn't want to go to trial,'' Amy replied. ''And, as you say, it would save time and expense.''

Robinette shook his head. ''There is no way we could go along with anything like that. Take the deal, Miss Schumacher. Believe me, it's a good one. Tell her, Mrs. Hamilton.''

''It isn't my case,'' Beth replied.

''Miss Schumacher?'' Robinette asked again.

''I'm sorry, Mr. Robinette, I'm sure it is a generous offer, but I simply can't accept it,'' Amy said.

Robinette stood there a moment longer, as if unable to believe she had turned him down. Then, recovering, he nodded to Amy and Beth. ''Good day, ladies. I'm sorry to have taken your time.''

Angered by Robinette's report of his meeting with the P.D., Stone picked up the phone and called Amy Schumacher, putting her voice on the speaker so Robinette could also hear.

"Miss Schumacher, Ben Stone here," he began.

"Ah, Mr. Stone, yes. Mr. Robinette would have, no doubt, reported back to you by now."

"He did, Miss Schumacher, and in fact he is here with me now."

"Hello, Miss Schumacher," Robinette said.

"Mr. Robinette," Amy replied.

"Miss Schumacher, I suppose you know the reason I'm calling," Stone said.

"I think I have an idea."

"I wanted to give you a chance to reconsider your response to our offer," Stone said. "I'm not sure you understand the generosity of this offer."

"Oh, I'm sure that by your standards it's quite generous," Amy replied. "And if I didn't have the confidence in this case that I do have, I would jump at it. But my client wants his day in court."

"Your client, or you, Miss Schumacher?"

"I beg your pardon?"

"You'll excuse me, but I have heard talk that you are a woman of, shall we say, ambition?"

"Do you have something against lawyers with ambition, counselor?" Amy asked coolly.

"It depends on whether your ambition helps or hurts your client."

"Your concern for Mr. Grisham's well-being is touching," Amy replied. "Perhaps I can tap into it during the trial. If you have nothing more, Mr. Stone, I do have work to do. I have a big case coming up.''

"Well, Miss Schumacher, what can I say except, 'I'll see you in court'?"

"I'm looking forward to it, Mr. Stone," Amy said.

Stone hung up, then looked over at Robinette. "I guess we'd better take the news to Adam."

Wentworth was sitting on the sofa in his office, drinking coffee and eating a doughnut.

"Umm, have you tried these?" he asked, offering the box. "They're from the new bakery that just opened down the street. They're the best doughnuts I've ever eaten."

Both Stone and Robinette took one.

"Have some coffee too," Adam offered.

Stone accepted the coffee, Robinette declined.

"So, how did the meeting go?" Wentworth asked. "I really hated to be so generous with this, but you were right—it's better to get it over with. I guess she jumped at the deal?"

"She turned us down, Adam," Stone said.

"What?" Wentworth asked, looking up in surprise.

"Flat," Stone added.

"What more could she want?"

"She wants the time served to be in a hospital, with release from the hospital to be decided upon by a psychiatric board," Robinette said.

"What is she, crazy?"

Stone nodded. "Yes, crazy with ambition. Right now I don't think there's any deal we could offer that she would find acceptable. She wants to get into that courtroom. She's auditioning for Thad Limbaugh, and we're convenient."

"And she's entered a plea of not guilty by reason of insanity?" Wentworth asked.

"Yes, well, let's get that sicko examined by our own expert. Have Elizabeth schedule a meeting for, what's his name . . . Grisham," Wentworth said.

"I've already called Dr. Olivet to see if she could handle it," Robinette replied. "She's adjusting her schedule."

"I want to take the gloves off on this one, Adam," Stone suggested. "I want a solid kill."

"Go for it," Wentworth replied, wiping his mouth with a napkin.

Superior Court, January 12

Judge Andrew J. Helgen was a big man with bushy, dark eyebrows and a full head of snow-white hair. He leaned forward on the bench and clasped his hands together, almost as if in prayer. He fixed a long gaze on the jury, then the gallery, and finally upon the counselors.

"All right," he said. "Everything seems to be in place here. The defense has entered a plea of not guilty, and not guilty by reason of insanity, is that correct?"

"That is correct, Your Honor," Amy said, rising to answer.

"Are you ready to begin?"

"Defense is ready, Your Honor."

"And the State of New York?"

"Prosecution is ready, Your Honor," Stone replied, also standing to give his answer.

"Very well," Judge Helgen said. "Prosecution, you may present your opening remarks."

Stone, still standing, walked around his table toward the jury box.

"Ladies and gentlemen of the jury, under normal circumstances the sole burden of proof falls upon the prosecution. The prosecution is required to prove to the jury—'beyond a reasonable doubt'—that a crime took place, and that the defendant committed that crime.

"We fully intend to do that. We will show you physical evidence to establish the fact that a murder did take place, and we will show you the physical evidence which will conclusively link Mr. Grisham to that murder. In addition, we will offer into evidence Mr. Grisham's sworn confession admitting that he did, indeed, commit the murder. That confession has neither been recanted nor challenged by the defense. Therefore, the burden of proof borne by the prosecution is an easy one. A murder *was* committed . . . and Bertis Grisham *did* commit it. These are indisputable, and undisputed, facts.

"But the very nature of this case has changed the ground rules under which our trial will proceed. Because, you see, the defense has entered a plea of not guilty, not from any dispute of the facts as we shall present them, but not guilty by reason of insanity. In other words, even though they freely admit that Mr. Grisham did kill Mary Stillman, they claim that he was insane at the time and, as a result of that insanity, was totally incapable of discerning right from wrong. Do you know what that means? That means that the Defense has taken the burden of proof upon their shoulder. Because in order to make their case, Defense must now *prove* to each of you—*beyond a reasonable doubt*—that Bertis Grisham did not know the difference between right and wrong.

"In any type of deductive reasoning, there are four categories of consideration. There is that which is impossible, that which is possible, that which is probable, and that which is known. But in order for the defense to meet its obligation in this case, you must disregard that which is impossible, that which is possible, and even that which is probable. The final verdict must be rendered only on the basis of what is *known.*

"Now, as you sit there in the jury box, what is irrefutably known? Well, what is known, even before the first word of testimony is heard, is that a murder *has* taken place. The victim of that brutal murder was Mary McCready Stillman. What is also known, even before the first word of testimony is heard, is that Bertis Grisham *did* commit that murder. These are facts, confessed to by Bertis Grisham.

"Defense is going to try and make the claim that while Bertis Grisham did, indeed, crush Mary Stillman's skull, he did not know that what he was doing was wrong. The reasonable assumption is that Grisham *did* know that it was wrong to murder Mary McCready. That is the premise under which this case will begin. And if the defense's argument is not compelling enough to convince you, *beyond all reasonable doubt,* to change your mind, then that is also the premise under which this case must end." Stone held up three fingers, then enumerated the final points. "A murder was committed, Bertis Grisham committed the murder, and Bertis Grisham knew that what he was doing was wrong."

When Stone took his seat, Robinette put his

hand on his shoulder and leaned over. "Good job, Ben," he said quietly.

"Miss Schumacher, have you any opening remarks?" Judge Helgen asked.

"Yes, Your Honor," Amy replied. She stood up and tugged once at the hem of the jacket of her cobalt-blue wool suit. To compliment the suit, she was wearing a red and white silk scarf at her neck. She knew that she looked good in the suit, but that wasn't the only reason she wore it. She intended, with the patriotic colors, to send a subliminal signal to the jurors.

Two of the male jurors were veterans of the Vietnam War. Also, one of the women on the jury had a son who had been killed in Vietnam. It was very important to Amy's case that these three jurors be included, and because neither Stone nor Robinette knew what she was looking for, they had not challenged those specific jurors.

"I wonder if any of you have visited the Vietnam War Memorial in Washington, D.C.?" Amy began. "If you haven't gone, you really should do so someday. It's very impressive, this huge, shining black slab, with all those silent names.

"You may remember that, at first, the wall was very controversial. Now, however, nearly everyone is universal in their praise. A totally unexpected and baffling phenomenon has developed in the way the wall affects people . . .

especially veterans of the war. To see a strong, middle-aged, gray-haired man standing there in front of the wall, weeping uncontrollably, is perhaps one of the most powerful examples I can think of, of what psychiatrists call post-traumatic stress disorder, or PTS.

"I say it is a powerful example because the men and women who took part in that war have come home and gone on to lead their own lives. They are doctors, lawyers, politicians, truck drivers, farmers, insurance salesmen, car dealers . . . you name it, they occupy every fabric of our society. In other words, they are normal, productive citizens. They are also our neighbors, friends, and relatives. I'm sure you would never think of one of them standing in front of a bank, or a supermarket, or a deli, weeping openly. And yet we have learned to accept those tears when we see them standing at the wall . . . face-to-face with their own reflection of their own image from that haunting list of names. There, at the wall, all of their pent-up emotions: sorrow, fear, love, loneliness, confusion, and yes, even the rejection they felt when they returned—all those emotions are psychologically released. Strong men weep, for they cannot prevent themselves from doing so.

"That is what PTS does to someone who has been subjected to a great emotional stress. PTS takes control of all reason, making a person do things that, under ordinary circumstances, he would never do. And now we are learning that although the Vietnam War gave us insight into PTS, it is not a disorder limited to those people who were in Vietnam. People who have been hostages exhibit such symptoms, as do people who are born, raised, and live in high-crime areas, afraid to leave their own homes after dark.

"Though Bertis Grisham is not a Vietnam veteran, he is, nevertheless, a warrior who has been exposed to years of emotional stress. Mr. Grisham is what we call an activist. Now, all of us know someone who is ardently committed to a cause . . . be it the civil rights or the peace movement of the sixties, or today's issues such as pro-choice or pro-life, women's rights, animal rights, the environment, hunger, homelessness, gun control, anti-smoking, AIDS Awareness, freedom of expression or obscenity. The list could go on and on and on, of course, and you may even espouse a cause that I didn't mention. But you, and most people, tend to select those one or two causes that are important to you . . . and then you generally support only one side of that cause."

Amy looked over at her client. "Mr. Grisham is such an activist, ladies and gentlemen, that he has demonstrated for all of those causes, and more. And here is something I think you will find fascinating. At one time or another Mr.

Grisham has demonstrated for both sides of the same issue. For example, he has been both pro-choice and pro-life. He has demonstrated for freedom of artistic expression, but he has also burned books and records he and others thought were objectionable. He has demonstrated for gun control, but he has also carried signs demanding that the right to bear arms be protected.

"But believe me, ladies and gentlemen, Mr. Grisham has paid the price for all his activism. He has been jeered, spat upon, pummeled with rocks and bricks, sprayed with high-pressure water hoses, beaten with billy clubs, tear-gassed, and jailed. As psychologists will tell you, such a life leaves a person scarred in body and soul."

Amy paused, then looked back toward the jury. "And he has done this for more than ten long years. Is Bertis Grisham a candidate for PTS? Of course he is. You cannot deny that fact unless you deny the existence of the disorder itself. Yes, Bertis Grisham did kill Mary Stillman, but he did not murder her, any more than a driver might murder someone in an unavoidable automobile accident. And, as those drivers often need psychiatric help to enable them to cope with the tragedy they have caused . . . so too will Bertis Grisham. All I ask of you is that, as this trial unfolds, you listen to the testimony and examine the evidence that will be presented to you, with a mind that is open to logic, reason, understanding, and compassion. If you do that, you will render the right verdict. Of that, I have no doubt."

As Amy returned to her seat, Judge Helgen looked over at the prosecutor's table.

"You may call your first witness," he said.

"Thank you, Your Honor," Robinette replied. "The State calls Jim Siffer."

Just as he had in the first trial, Jim Siffer testified that he was the first on the scene and was the one who discovered the body under the sheets of corrugated metal. He added to this testimony, however, the fact that he had seen Bertis Grisham many times, hanging around the construction site. Amy had no questions.

Dr. Baker gave substantially the same testimony he had given in the first trial. He described in gory detail the irregular deforming wound that involved the lateral aspect of the orbit, brow, and the right maxilla, extending from the extreme right forehead to the level of the nasolabial fold. He also pointed out the fact that the cavity of the frontal sinus could be seen through the opening of the wound. This was graphic evidence of the severity of the beating.

During the questioning, it was brought out that Dr. Baker's initial belief had been that whoever killed Mary Stillman must have been left-handed, because the crushing blow as to the right side of the victim's head.

Amy had no questions of the witness.

The police officer who had delivered the scrapings from the wound to the forensic lab testified that the evidence had been in his control and in his sight for the entire operation so that there was absolutely no question as to the possibility of any part of the evidence being tampered with or switched.

Amy had no questions of the witness.

Paulie Margolis was the next witness. His testimony told how the murder weapon had been found. He added that he suspected what it was from the moment he saw it, and therefore was very careful not to touch it nor let any of his men touch it. When the police took the pipe out of the hole, it had not been disturbed since the person who used it dropped it.

Amy had no questions of the witness.

Dan Fenton, the forensic expert, testified on the physical evidence. He identified the foreign matter that was taken from the victim's wound and matched it, perfectly, with the water pipe found at the site, thus conclusively identifying it as the murder weapon. He also described how he had lifted the fingerprints from the iron pipe and explained how they had managed to survive exposure to the elements for the several weeks the pipe lay undiscovered.

Stone questioned him specifically about the fact that turpentine was found in the wound.

"How much turpentine did you find?" Stone asked.

"Very little."

"Tell me about the cloth that was found with the murder weapon. What did you find on it?"

"A great deal of blood which matched the victim's blood, both in type and in DNA. There was also a lot of dirt and some microscopic elements of oil-saturated sawdust."

"Sawdust?"

"Commercial floor sweep," Fenton explained. "It was a product which janitors used to use to clean wooden floors. They would put it down, then sweep up again with big push brooms. Because of the oil saturation, the sawdust would pick up dirt and dust and leave a sheen on the floor. It was very popular for a long time, but it isn't used much anymore because it is a fire hazard."

"What does that suggest to you?" Stone asked.

"It suggests that the cloth was used to wipe blood up from a floor that had, at sometime in its history, been subjected to floor sweep."

"Was there any turpentine on the cloth? Could that have been used to clean up the blood?"

"No," Fenton replied. "There was no turpentine on the cloth. The only place I found turpentine was in the wound itself.''

"Thank you," Stone said. "Your witness, Miss Schumacher."

"I have no questions, Your Honor," Amy said without even looking up from the notes she was taking on the tablet.

Detective Mike Logan was the next witness. He described how he matched the fingerprints on the murder weapon with Bertis Grisham's prints. He explained how it was confusing to them at first, because Bertis Grisham was supposed to have spent the night in the detention cell at the Midtown South Precinct. Then he told how they learned, when they called, that it wasn't Grisham who spent that night in jail, but someone else who had given Grisham's name.

Logan then explained how they tracked Grisham down and how, when they found him participating in yet another demonstration, he tried to run.

Amy had no questions of Detective Logan.

Detective Sergeant Cerreta was next. Cerreta took Grisham's confession, and Stone asked him to now read the confession into the record. Cerreta began to read, covering the opening business of establishing Grisham's name, address, the time and date of the statement, and the location where the statement was being taken.

QUESTION: Did you kill Mary Stillman?

ANSWER: Yes, I did.

QUESTION: Would you describe the weapon you used?

ANSWER: It was a heavy piece of iron, a bar or a pipe or something, I'm not sure which. I picked it up from a pile of scrap there where they were tearing down the hotel.

QUESTION: How did you use the weapon?

ANSWER: I hit her with it.

QUESTION: How many times did you hit her?

ANSWER: I'm not sure. Many times. I just kept hitting until there was no—you know—feedback to my blows. Instead of hitting something hard, it was like I was hitting into a piece of rotten fruit or something.

QUESTION: After the beating, what did you do with the weapon?

ANSWER: I already had figured out what I was going to do with it. Earlier, I had seen some forms where they were about to pour concrete. I dropped it down there. I didn't think it would ever be found.

QUESTION: Why did you kill Mrs. Stillman, Mr. Grisham?

ANSWER: Because of who she was . . . and what she was.

QUESTION: Could you be more specific?

ANSWER: She was Mary McCready Stillman, a member of one of the wealthiest families in the city. And she was also Queen Mary, one of the homeless. It was a perfect marriage of the two opposite extremes of our society, and a beautiful example of what is wrong. She had to be killed, don't you see? Mary McCready Stillman was a sacrifice to our age, like John Kennedy and Martin Luther King were sacrifices to their age. And, like Lee Harvey Oswald and James Earl Ray, I have merely put things into motion. We have, each of us, played a vital role for our country.

QUESTION: Are you saying that Oswald and Ray did something good for our country?

ANSWER: Good? No, they did no good, they did only evil. But don't you understand? Through their evil deeds, the greatness of Kennedy and King has been preserved for the ages. There is a symbiosis between good and evil . . . one cannot exist without the other. For the greater good of society, I am willing to play whatever role fate has chosen for me.

QUESTION: And you believe fate chose you to kill Mrs. Stillman?

ANSWER: Yes.

QUESTION: Would you describe the process by which you put that fate into motion?

ANSWER: I would be glad to. Actually, you have to understand that Mary Stillman was a dead woman from the moment I found out who she was.

QUESTION: How is it that you knew who she was?

ANSWER: I made an effort to befriend her, even though she was friendly with nobody else. She told me all about herself . . . who she was and who her family was. At first, I didn't believe her, but I asked around and found out that Arthur Stillman's wife really had disappeared a long time ago. She used to talk to me about riding. She said she was quite a good rider when she was a young woman. She said she almost made it to the Olympics, and she showed me a picture of herself as a young woman, on a horse. I went down to the newspaper and looked up in the society pages when Arthur Stillman was married and, sure enough, the picture of the bride, Mary McCready, was the same woman as the woman on the horse in the picture Mary had.

After that, I pretended that I too was interested in riding, and I went to the library and read everything I could about it so I could discuss it with her.

QUESTION: You were winning her confidence?

ANSWER: Yes, that is exactly what I was doing. And it worked too. Would you like to know how well it worked?

QUESTION: How well did it work?

ANSWER: I am the one who talked her into going to see her husband and her brother to try and get the new construction stopped. She hadn't even thought of it.

QUESTION: Did you really think she could talk her husband into suspending the construction?

ANSWER: I knew she wouldn't be successful. But I hoped that it would come out that he was tearing down the building where she lived. That would bring attention to it, don't you see? Only it never came out in the papers that she had gone to see him.

QUESTION: What did you do next?

ANSWER: That's when I started looking for the opportunity to kill her. Then, when I saw her brother go into the Avery Building, I knew I had to act that very day. So I gave a friend one hundred dollars to get himself picked up for impeding the flow of traffic, then pass himself off as me. I knew that for a misdemeanor like that they wouldn't check any closer . . . and that would give me the perfect alibi.

I couldn't be connected with the killing if I was in jail.

I watched the building until McCready left, then I picked up a piece of iron from the scrap heap on the corner and went into Mary's room. I thought Mary would still be there, and I was going to kill her and leave her. But she wasn't in her room, so I went to look for her. That was when I saw her talking to her brother in front of the kitchen.

QUESTION: What did you do next?

ANSWER: I waited until the conversation was finished, then I followed her. I was going to kill her right there, but one of the other women from the building, the one they call Lucy Goosey, showed up, so I had to hide. By then I had no choice. I had to follow her on into the building. I called to her just before she started up the steps, and told her that her husband was here to see her. I told her that he had changed his mind, that he was going to stop the new construction. She came back to see him, and when she got close enough, I hit her. [Here the witness chuckles] I hit her with a left-handed swing because I knew that her brother was left-handed. After I was sure she was dead, I found a piece of cloth and used it to wipe up the blood from the floor. Then I dragged her body over and hid it in the corner of the room.

QUESTION: You left the body in the lobby of the Avery Building?

ANSWER: Yeah. But then later, I got to thinking that it would be better if the body was found on the very site where Stillman Towers was being built, so, in the middle of the night I came back and moved it. That's also when I dropped a couple of drops of turpentine into where I bashed open her head.

QUESTION: Why did you do that?

ANSWER: I knew that her brother was an artist, and I knew that I wasn't the only one who had seen them together. I also knew that artists use turpentine, and I knew that the police would examine everything real close. I was pretty sure they would make the connection. [Here, the witness chuckles again] The turpentine and the idea about killing her left-handed almost worked. McCready went to trial. It would have worked too, if the concrete had been poured when it was supposed to.

QUESTION: You are talking about the concrete that would have covered the murder weapon?

ANSWER: Yes.

QUESTION: Have you anything else to add, Mr. Grisham?

ANSWER: No.

QUESTION: Do you have any remorse or misgivings?

ANSWER: I am an instrument of fate. One cannot have remorse over being chosen as an instrument of fate.

QUESTION: Was there any coercion on the part of any police officer or member of the police department to get you to make this statement?

ANSWER: No.

QUESTION: Were you promised anything, any leniency or reduced sentence, for making this statement?

ANSWER: No.

QUESTION: Have you made this statement of your own will and volition?

ANSWER: Yes.

Cerreta looked up at Stone. "That's all of it," he said.

"Detective Cerreta, since you took that statement, has Mr. Grisham made any effort to change any of it, or to recant all or any part of it?"

"No."

"As far as you know, the statement he made to you and which you just read to the jury, still stands, unaltered, as his declaration of the facts and circumstances surrounding the killing of Mary Stillman?"

"Yes."

"Thank you, Sergeant, no further questions."

"Miss Schumacher?" Judge Helgen asked.

"Defense has no wish to challenge the statement as read, Your Honor," Amy said.

"Your Honor, Detective Cerreta was the final prosecution witness. Prosecution rests."

"Very well, Mr. Stone," Judge Helgen said. He looked at his watch, then at Amy. "I assume your witnesses will be psychiatrists and the like?"

"Yes, Your Honor."

"Well, knowing how long those people like to talk, I wouldn't want to have to put a crimp in his testimony by breaking it for lunch. So, let's go ahead and break now, but be back here promptly at one."

* * *

Amy ate lunch at a deli just down the street from the courthouse. She was joined at her table by Thad Limbaugh, who had been watching the trial from the gallery.

"I thought your opening statement was brilliant," Limbaugh said. "If you handle the rest of your case as well as you did that, you will be an easy sell to my partners."

Amy spread brown mustard on her pastrami, then looked up at Limbaugh with a big smile. "What if I win?"

Limbaugh chuckled. "Ah, the optimism of youth," he said. "You know, I once read that when Joe Namath was playing football, he expected every play he called to be a touchdown. I think greatness comes from such self-confidence. Providing, of course, that you aren't so destroyed by the occasional setbacks that you eventually lose your effectiveness. You don't understand, my dear. Whether you win or lose this case makes no difference to your future with Sidwell, Potashnick and Limbaugh."

"No, you don't understand, Mr. Limbaugh," Amy said. "I am going to win this case . . . perhaps not in the way you think, but it's a lock. Trust me on this."

As Amy Schumacher was having lunch with her future employer, Stone and Robinette were eating Chinese, brought in to their office so they could go over their notes. Wentworth stuck his head in.

"Ben, Paul," he said. "Come in here, you might want to see this."

Stone and Robinette followed Wentworth into his office, where the TV was playing.

"I was just catching the noon news," he said. "They teased the next story . . . ah, here it comes."

"Hence Fielding took delivery of another deserted building today, promising that, within six months, the building will be completely renovated and occupied by needy families. Our Jeanie Bennett is on the scene."

The picture switched from the studio to the street. A large building could be seen in the background, obviously deserted. The camera panned down to show an attractive black female reporter standing between two men. One was Hence Fielding, the other was Arthur Stillman.

"John, the spirit of brotherhood and community betterment is alive and well in New York, as shown by these two gentlemen. The man to my left is Hence Fielding, founder and president of FACE-IT. The gentleman to my right should certainly need no introduction to New Yorkers, or to anyone else in America. This is developer and entrepreneur, Arthur Stillman. Mr. Fielding, I'll begin with you. What, exactly, is going on here?"

The camera panned to a one-shot of Hence Fielding.

"*The building you see here is the old Milnot Hotel. It was quite a fine hotel in its day, though its day passed long ago. It was slated for destruction, but when the construction engineers took a closer look at it, they found that its basic structure was sound. In other words, it is an ideal candidate for renovation and rehabilitation. I made a personal visit and appeal to Mr. Stillman and . . . well, perhaps we should let Mr. Stillman finish the story.*"

The picture shifted to Arthur Stillman.

"*When Hence came to me with the proposal that I donate this building to FACE-IT, my first reaction was negative. Then I began thinking of my late wife. It is no secret, of course, that she was recently murdered, because her murder has spawned two highly public trials. Mary and I had been estranged for many, many years, but I still felt a sense of compassion for her, and I feel strongly that this is something she would want me to do.*"

"*Mr. Stillman, you'll excuse the question, sir, but what do you say to those critics who might say that you are too late in showing your compassion?*"

"*I would remind them of the biblical parable of the workers in the field, where those who came last were paid the same measure as those who came first. Or, to put it more bluntly, better late than never. I wish, of course, that I had seen the opportunity to do this before the tragic circumstances which took my wife's life, but I cannot change the past. I can, however, honor her in this way.*"

"Mr. Fielding, this question is for you. How soon will the apartments be occupied?"

"I would think within a very few months. I have already made arrangements to secure the material needed, as well as the Title 8 loans."

"Thank you, Mr. Stillman, Mr. Fielding. This is Jeanie Bennett."

Wentworth snapped the picture off. "Stillman will get a two million dollar tax write-off, Fielding will make another two million, and they're being paraded around as the great saviors of mankind," he growled.

"If you ask me, Fielding is the one who should be on trial," Stone said.

Wentworth chuckled and held up his hand. "No, thank you," he said. "One trial at a time. And no more trials for this case, if you don't mind."

"We won't need any more," Stone said. "This one is going our way, and even Schumacher knows it. All she's trying to do is make a splash."

"And Thad Limbaugh is sitting right there taking it all in," Robinette added.

"Yes," Wentworth said. "But let's make certain all our t's are crossed and our i's dotted, okay? I don't want this one overturned on some technicality we might overlook."

"Paul, we'd better get back," Stone said.

glancing at his watch. "Judge Helgen said one o'clock, and he means one."

Supreme Court of New York, Afternoon Session

As her first witness, Amy called Dr. Alvin Westlake. She spent first several minutes drawing out his qualifications. In addition to being a practicing psychiatrist, Westlake was a professor of psychiatry and the author of a best-selling book entitled: *PTS: A Time Bomb in Our Midst.*

"And now, Dr. Westlake," Amy began, "would you explain PTS to the court?"

"Oh, my dear young lady," Dr. Westlake complained. "You are asking me to explain in a few moments what it takes an entire semester to teach. And that to students who already have a background in psychology."

"Then pretend this is a question in Psych 101," Amy suggested. "And explain it the best you can."

Dr. Westlake leaned forward and raised a finger, as if he were giving a classroom lecture. "The essential feature of PTS disorder is the onset of characteristic symptoms. The symptoms follow an event whose degree of distress is far beyond the range of common experiences. This includes such normal stress-inducing events as bereavement, chronic illness, business losses, or marital conflict.''

"Nearly everyone has been through one or more of those experiences, Doctor, the loss of a loved one, divorce, etcetera," Amy said. "It is natural to feel depression at such times, is it not?''

"Oh, yes, quite natural. In fact it would be unnatural not to feel depression at such times.''

"So that I, and the jury, can understand just what you are saying . . . these depressions, even severe depressions, would not trigger PTS?''

"No.''

"Doctor, in my opening remarks to the jury, I suggested that ex-Vietnam soldiers who weep in front of the wall may be suffering from PTS. I got that idea from your book. I didn't misunderstand you, did I?''

"No, you didn't misunderstand. By now nearly everyone has known, or has heard of, Vietnam veterans who have had a difficult time in readjusting. Even now, going on thirty years after the fact, these veterans are still presenting symptoms. Though it had not been diagnosed as such, the same thing was true as far back as the Civil War. I believe a very good case could be made that the lawlessness of such groups as

Jesse James and his gang was due to PTS. We saw it again after World War One, World War Two, and Korea. We have done a better job of identifying it with the Vietnam veterans.''

"Surely, Doctor, you aren't comparing an outlaw like Jesse James with those men who weep at the Vietnam Memorial?'' Amy asked.

"Yes, I am, as a matter of fact. Of course, the degree of the condition varies. Some have adjusted to the trauma so well that they don't even know it exists. They can, and do, live perfectly normal and productive lives. It is only when they encounter a certain triggering mechanism —such as the emotional experience of visiting the wall and coming face-to-face with the names of all their peers who did not come back from the war—that they temporarily lose control.''

"Is war the only thing that will cause a person to experience PTS?'' Amy asked.

"Not at all. Stressors which will produce PTS include natural disasters such as flood or earthquakes, airplane crashes, or large fires, as well as deliberately-caused disasters such as bombing, torture, or incarceration.''

"You said there are various degrees of severity. Would this have anything to do with how the trauma is brought on?''

"Absolutely. The disorder is more severe and longer-lasting when the stressor is of human design, such as unjust incarceration, or deliberate torture or murder. Prisoner-of-war camps and, of course, the Nazi concentration camps are perfect examples of that.''

"You mean," Amy said, "someone observing examples of man's inhumanity to man will suffer more severely than someone who has been affected by, say, an act of God, such as a hurricane or earthquake?''

"Yes, that is correct.''

"What are the symptoms of PTS?''

"In its mildest form, one has a vague feeling of depression, or an uncontrollable urge to weep.''

"What would be it's most severe form?''

"In its most severe form, the reduced capacity for modulation may express itself in unpredictable explosions of violence.''

"How violent?''

"There is no limiting factor.''

"Tell me, Doctor," Amy said, "what do you mean by the term, 'reduced capacity for modulation'?''

"It means an inability to adjust to certain situations, which could lead to periods of uncontrolled activity.''

"Might one kill, during this period of uncontrolled activity?''

"Oh, there have been many examples of that, all the way back to and including the aforementioned Jesse James.''

"You have examined my client, haven't you, Doctor?"

"Yes, I have had at least three extended sessions with him."

"Have you made a diagnosis of his condition?"

"Yes, I have."

"And what is that diagnosis?"

"I would definitely say that he is suffering from post-traumatic stress disorder. This is most evident in his diminished responsiveness, manifested by emotional anesthesia. For example, the way he was able to describe the actual incident in such cold, clinical terms . . . such as: 'I just kept hitting until there was no feedback to my blows. Instead of hitting something hard, it was like I was hitting into rotten fruit or something.' And his statement that he felt no remorse. Bertis Grisham has a history of concern for the welfare of others. That he is so detached from the brutality and inhumanity of what he did, is, in my opinion, compelling evidence that he is in the throes of an anxiety disorder."

"How was this disorder introduced, Doctor?" Amy asked.

"You covered that quite well, I thought, in your opening remarks," Westlake replied. "Mr. Grisham has indeed been in a war—a 'street war,' as it were—for over ten years. During that time, he has seen extreme examples of suffering, hunger, and neglect. In addition Mr. Grisham has been subjected to frequent periods of incarceration, which to him would seem unjust because his only violation was to follow the dictates of his conscience. He has also been beaten, hosed, and gassed. He is a prime example of what I call in my book, 'PTS, the Urban Equation,' or PTS-UE.''

"One final question, Doctor. In your opinion, is the anxiety disorder under which Bertis Grisham is suffering, severe enough to bring on one of those bouts of uncontrolled violence?''

"Yes. As I have already stated, the killing of Mary Stillman is totally foreign to Bertis Grisham's behavioral history. If he had not been in the grip of PTS-UE, this killing would have never taken place.''

"Thank you, Doctor. Your witness.''

Stone walked over toward the jury box, then turned toward Westlake.

"Doctor, would a person such as you describe understand the difference between right and wrong?''

"It wouldn't matter.''

"Oh, but it does matter. Bear in mind, Doctor, that we are looking for the legal definition of insanity—not a clinical diagnosis. If Grisham had the capacity to differentiate between right and wrong, then he was not, legally, insane.''

"It would not make any difference whether

or not he understood the difference between right or wrong. In such a state he would be absolutely unable to control his behavior."

"Doctor, this PTS-UE that you mentioned. Is it a generally recognized disorder? Would one find it in the *Diagnostic and Statistical Manual of Mental Disorders*?"

"Uh, no, it isn't listed in the *DSM*."

"But it is in your book, *PTS: A Time Bomb in Our Midst*?"

"Yes, it's in Chapter Eight."

"Your book sold very well, didn't it, Doctor?"

"Yes, I'm pleased to say, it did sell very well."

"In fact, it was on the best-seller charts in *Publishers Weekly* for twenty-six weeks, I believe?"

"In hardcover," Westlake replied. "It was forty-five weeks in paperback."

"What was your readership, Doctor? Was it used as a textbook?"

"No. Textbooks don't generate that kind of numbers."

"Your book was well-received by the general public. But to be honest about it, Doctor, it wasn't received that well among your peers, was it?"

"There is always bound to be a certain amount of protectionism and jealousy among professionals," Westlake defended.

Stone walked back over to his table and

picked up a folder. "I don't want to embarrass you, Doctor, but I have several reviews here—"

"Objection! Your Honor, we aren't here to discuss Dr. Westlake's literary skills, we are only concerned with his diagnosis," Amy said.

"Your Honor, these aren't literary reviews," Stone replied. "Actually, the literary reviews were quite good. These are reviews by members of the American Psychiatric Association, which go to the accuracy of the psychology. If Dr. Westlake is going to quote his book as expert source material for his diagnosis, then we should have a right to challenge that book."

"Objection overruled."

"As I was saying, Doctor, I don't want to embarrass you. But without reading these reviews aloud, would you agree with me that others in your field refer to this book as 'pop psychology'?"

"There is nothing wrong with pop psychology," Dr. Westlake defended. "If it helps the lay person to understand."

"I don't deny that, Doctor," Stone said. "But we are in a court of law. And while I realize that psychology is far from an exact science, we must, at least, demand as exacting an interpretation of the existing science as we can. Now in truth, Doctor, there is no such disorder as PTS-UE, is there?"

"Just because the disorder hasn't been catalogued in the *DSM*, doesn't mean that the disorder doesn't exist."

"Doctor, I am told there are millions of species of insects that have not yet been identified. That doesn't mean they don't exist . . . but in a court of law we cannot discuss the needle-nosed milk bug, because there is no record of such a bug. By that same token, Doctor, we cannot discuss PTS-UE."

"Withdraw the designator *U.E.* and we still have a patient who is suffering from post-traumatic stress. I stand by my original diagnosis."

"Doctor, you heard Grisham's statement read, how he planned the murder so carefully as to set up his alibi, strike the victim with left-handed blows, and even drop turpentine into the wound. It was, in fact, so brilliantly conceived that the state actually went to trial with the man Grisham framed. Would someone who is suffering from mental illness be capable of such detailed and brilliant planning?"

Dr. Westlake smiled. "Mr. Stone, there is a story that every first-year psychology student hears. It seems—"

"Excuse me, Doctor, I don't wish to be rude, but would someone who is suffering from mental illness be capable of such detailed and brilliant planning? Yes or no?"

"Yes, I believe he would."

"Thank you, Doctor. No further questions."

Amy stood up. "Doctor, during our first meeting, I asked you the same question Mr. Stone just asked, didn't I?"

"Yes."

"And you answered me with the same story you were about to tell?"

"Yes."

"Would you tell it please, Doctor? It did a lot to convince me. . . . I think it might help the jury to understand."

"Yes, thank you. The story is that there was a motorist who had a flat tire on the street in front of a mental institution. During the course of changing the tire, he inadvertently kicked all four lug nuts down the storm drain. When that happened, he was totally stumped as to what he should do. There was a patient just on the other side of the fence who had been watching.

" 'Don't worry,' the patient said. 'Just take one lug nut off each of the other three wheels. That will secure your wheel until you can get to a service station and buy new lug nuts.'

" 'Why, that's brilliant,' the motorist said. 'But you are a mental patient. How did you ever come up with such an idea?'

" 'Look,' the patient explained. 'I'm in here because I'm crazy—not because I'm stupid.' "

The gallery, and the jury, laughed.

"Thank you, Doctor," Amy concluded.

After Dr. Westlake, there followed a host of

other witnesses, men and women who had known Grisham over the years and who had demonstrated with him in the past. The witnesses were united in their praise of Grisham's gentleness and humanity. All expressed shock that he could have killed anyone, and all insisted that he would never have done such a thing if he had been "in his right mind."

Stone then called as a rebuttal witness, to Dr. Westlake's testimony, Dr. Elizabeth Olivet. Having been an expert witness for the D.A. many times before, her qualifications were quickly established.

"Dr. Olivet, you had the opportunity to examine the defendant, did you not?"

"Yes, I interviewed him."

"In your opinion, is he, by the legal definition of the term, insane?"

"No."

"Does he, in fact, suffer from post-traumatic stress?"

"In my opinion, he does not. During our talk he displayed none of the associated features which are characteristic of PTS. He has no failing memory, no difficulty in concentration, and he has made no attempt to avoid the stress. On the contrary, by joining the AIDS demonstration immediately after his violent event, he reemersed himself in the same kind of stress which supposedly brought on his disorder in the first place. This is totally contrary to the pattern most often exhibited by PTS, which is to take extreme measures to avoid similar situations.''

"Does he suffer from any type of anxiety disorder?"

"If I were going to diagnose him, I would say there is an adjustment disorder. This is manifested in the way he constantly seeks some identity with first one cause and then another."

"Is this adjustment disorder of sufficient severity to bring on what Dr. Westlake calls 'reduced capacity for modulation'?"

"No," Olivet replied. "Adjustment disorder is much less severe than PTS, and is well within the range of common experience. Many well-adjusted people go through this."

"Would someone with this disorder know the difference between right and wrong?"

"Yes, of course."

"Would someone with this disorder be compelled to commit an act of violence over which they had no control?"

"No."

"Is it your expert opinion that Bertis Grisham is emotionally and mentally responsible for his actions?"

"That is my opinion, yes."

"Thank you, Doctor. No further questions."

"You had one interview with my client?" Amy asked, as she began her cross examination.

"Yes."

"Only one?"

"Yes, only one."

"Dr. Olivet . . . let's see, that is Ph.D., is it not? You are not a medical doctor?"

"No, I'm not."

"That would make you a psychologist, rather than a psychiatrist?"

"Yes."

"Don't misunderstand me, Doctor," Amy said. "I have all the respect in the world for your position and your expertise in the field. But don't psychologists deal somewhat more with mental disorders in general, than with specific patients?"

"We also do individual counseling."

"Counseling, yes, but aren't there sometimes nuances . . . subtleties, which only a medical doctor, who is attuned to both the physical as well as the psychological makeup of a patient, would be able to determine?"

"There has been no suggestion that any sort of physical insult may be the cause of Mr. Grisham's condition," Olivet replied.

"You had one—I believe you called it an interview—with my client. Dr. Westlake, a psychiatrist, had three, extended medical examinations and psychological evaluations of his patient. Under the circumstances, Doctor, wouldn't you say that Dr. Westlake is in a better position to form an opinion?''

"With all due respect to Dr. Westlake's acknowledged expertise in the field, I have examined many more subjects for a legal analysis of their condition than he has. Of the two of us, I feel that I am more qualified to make that specific judgment.''

"And so now the student is teaching the teacher?'' Amy asked.

"I beg your pardon?''

"You have taken classes from Dr. Westlake, have you not? In fact, you took two postgraduate classes from him.''

"Yes.''

Amy picked up a piece of paper from her table. "This is a student evaluation sheet of Dr. Westlake's class, containing your comments.''

"Objection,'' Stone said. "We have already accepted Dr. Westlake's credentials.''

"And began immediately to undermine them,'' Amy replied. "Your Honor, I would like the jury to know Dr. Olivet's opinion of Dr. Westlake, away from the heat of courtroom battle.''

"Objection overruled. You may read the evaluation comments.''

"Thank you, Your Honor. And now, reading, 'Dr. Westlake is clearly ahead of anyone else in the field of disorder diagnosis. He is breaking new ground in areas, which, until now, were only seen through intriguing glimpses. I shall be proud to claim in all future vitae, alumniship from the Dr. Westlake Institute of Diagnostics.' And there is another one, just as glowing, which I won't read. You did write this evaluation, didn't you?"

"Yes, I did."

"Has your opinion of Dr. Westlake changed?"

"We're dealing with apples and oranges here," Olivet replied.

"No we aren't, Miss Olivet. What we are dealing with is your evaluation of Dr. Westlake's ability to make a diagnosis. Do you feel, as you stated, that he is breaking new ground in the field of disorder diagnosis?"

"Yes, but—"

"Thank you, Doctor, that is all."

"Dr. Olivet, I believe you wanted to qualify your answer?" Stone said, opening his redirect.

"Yes," Olivet said.

"Please, feel free to do so now."

"I meant what I said in those evaluation sheets. I had, and I still have, all the respect in the world for Dr. Westlake. And I truly believe that he is breaking new ground in disorder diagnosis. But when I said apples and oranges, I was referring to the fact that, in a court of law, we must put certain structures and guidelines upon those diagnoses. There is, of course, no psychological or medical term 'insane.' That is purely a legal term. And the field of exploratory diagnostics, in which the entire nation acknowledges Dr. Westlake to be a pioneer, does not lend itself to these legal structures. It is like saying that because someone is an accomplished musician he must also be an excellent painter. That simply isn't so. But a lack in one does not lessen the skill in the other. Dr. Westlake is a brilliant diagnostician, but he is on the cutting edge of the field. This is a court of law. We must stay within bounds. There is no room here for experimentation."

"Thank you, Doctor. I have no further questions," Stone concluded.

During Stone's redirect, a bailiff brought a note to Robinette. When Stone sat down, Robinette showed him the note.

Ben, ask for an immediate meeting in the judge's chambers. Something urgent has come up.

Adam

"Your Honor, may I approach the bench?"

Judge Helgen nodded.

"What's this about, Ben?" the judge asked when Stone was before him.

"I have no idea, Your Honor. All I know is I

have a note from the District Attorney asking for an immediate consultation with you in your chambers. He showed the note to the judge.

"All right," the judge said. He struck the gavel. "Court is recessed for one-half hour. Miss Schumacher, I will be meeting with the prosecution in my chambers."

"Your Honor, is there—"

"You will be apprised, Miss Schumacher, if I think it is something you should know," Judge Helgen said.

"Thank you," Amy said. "We shall wait, patiently." She turned then and smiled, pointedly, at Thad Limbaugh.

"Did you see the way she smiled at Limbaugh?" Stone whispered to Robinette. "I didn't like the looks of that."

"What do you think it is, Ben? Do you think she's about to ambush us?"

"I don't know, but if we were in the Old West, I'd be watching my back about now."

Stone and Robinette followed the judge through the back door of the courtroom and down the hall to a small office. There, Adam Wentworth paced nervously.

"Adam, what is it?" Stone asked.

"We have a serious problem here," Wentworth said. "If the case doesn't go well, Defense will have a perfect grounds for appeal."

"Appeal? On what grounds?" Stone asked.

"Paul, when you went to speak to Amy Schumacher at her office, did you meet a Beth Hamilton?"

"Yes," Robinette said. "She shares an office with Schumacher."

"Uh-huh. And was she, by any chance, helping Schumacher prepare her defense?"

"Yes, she was."

Wentworth groaned.

"Adam, you want to tell me what in the Sam Hill this is all about?"

"According to my sources, Amy Schumacher has just learned who Beth Hamilton really is."

"Who is she?" Stone asked.

"Elizabeth Stillman."

Stone gasped. "The victim's daughter?"

"One and the same."

"And she was helping defend the man who murdered her mother?"

"Yes. And Paul knew it. Schumacher is going to be able to claim that she depended upon Miss Hamilton's assistance but now has reason to believe that that assistance may have been colored by personal considerations on the part of Beth Hamilton."

"I had no idea that was Elizabeth Stillman," Robinette defended.

"What I don't understand is how it is that Amy Schumacher didn't know?" Stone asked. "She worked with her."

"For reasons of her own, Beth Hamilton has been extremely secretive about her identity. I don't imagine any more than two or three people in the entire legal system of the city know who she is."

"How did Schumacher find out?" Stone asked.

"Who knows? She is an enterprising young woman," Wentworth replied.

"How was Paul supposed to know?"

"Mr. Stone, it doesn't matter whether Mr. Robinette knew or not," Judge Helgen said. "The appearance is all that is needed. I'm going to have to declare a mistrial."

"Now? But we're down to closing arguments, for chrissake!" Stone objected.

"Mistrial now, or verdict overturned later," Judge Helgen said. "I may as well save us the time and expense."

"Cut a deal, Ben," Adam said. "We aren't going to go through this again."

"It's not going to be a good deal for our side," Stone replied. "We aren't even looking at Man Two now. More than likely it'll be Reckless Homicide, and there will be little or no time."

"Cut a deal. Even if we have to do supervised probation and community service. Cut a deal. We have other cases on our plate."

Stone sighed. "All right, Adam, I'll talk to

Schumacher." He started toward the door, then stopped.

"Damnit," he said. "That's why she smiled at Limbaugh as we were leaving the courtroom."

"What are you talking about?" Wentworth asked.

"Miss Schumacher knew exactly what she was doing. We were set up."

"What can I tell you, Ben? It's just as I said, this is the year of the woman."

THE COMPELLING COURTROOM CLASSIC BY WHICH ALL OTHERS ARE JUDGED!

Anatomy of a Murder

Robert Traver

"Dramatic fireworks...Traver writes with gusto, with a mildly ribald sense of humor, with unflagging invention and narrative pace....Racy and rousing."

—*The New York Times*

"This is no mere courtroom novel but an enormously detailed and endlessly absorbing account of what a brilliant criminal lawyer thought and did."

—*Chicago Sunday Tribune*

Frank Galvin, a smart Irishman from the tough side of town, is the star litigator at a blue-chip Boston law firm. But the irresistible lure of a beautiful woman with a devastating secret threatens his hard-won acceptance by "the establishment."

Suddenly, Frank finds himself on the wrong side of a ferocious legal war—hired to destroy the people he trusts, loyal to those he doesn't. He's facing the biggest choice of his career—and the ultimate battle between duty and honor.

Caught in the crossfire of sexual temptation and murder, he'll call on the same unorthodox methods that made things sizzle in *The Verdict*. But this time, Galvin's got a lot more at stake, because winning the case could mean losing everything.

BARRY REED
THE CHOICE

"Better than *Presumed Innocent*!"

—*The Washington Post*

Four years ago, she was a vibrant young woman who came to give birth to her third child and instead left condemned to a deathlike, vegetative state for the rest of her life. The doctors at Boston's most prestigious Catholic hospital called it an unavoidable act of God. Veteran lawyer Frank Galvin knows it's negligence. And he's suing, for fifteen million dollars.

Up against the all-powerful Church and an unforgiving medical establishment, Galvin's reckless enough to resist the payoffs and keen enough to smell a cover-up. He's not doing it to resuscitate a career on the skids. He's not doing it for the law. He's doing it for justice—the kind hard won in the courtroom, and burned deep in the soul.

Inspiration for the Academy Award-nominated film starring Paul Newman, as well as Barry Reed's masterful sequel, *The Choice*, *The Verdict* is courtroom drama that's even more compelling on the printed page than on the movie screen.

THE VERDICT

Barry Reed